Richard Mann • Those Jackson County Blues

Bibliographic Information of the German National Library
The German National Library has registered this publication in the German
National Bibliography; detailed bibliographic information can be found online at
http://dnb.d-nb.de.
© Frieling-Verlag Berlin: A trademark of Frieling & Huffmann GmbH & Co. KG Phone: 0 30 /
766 999-0
www.frieling.de

Cover illustration: Emilia Agovic
Image source: pixabay
1st Edition 2021
ISBN (print) 978-3-8280-3648-2
ISBN (e-book) 978-3-8280-3649-9
All rights reserved Printed in Germany

Richard Mann

Those
Jackson County
Blues

FRIELING

In Memorium

Bob Allen Howard †1975

Steve Hollie † 1975

Thomas Evans † 1975

"Death is a distant rumor to the young."
- Andrew A. Rooney

"Death never comes at the right time,
despite what we mortals believe.
Death comes like a thief."
- Christopher Pike

- Some of the names in this book are completely fictional -

Contents

Prelude

Later in life he would spontaneously remember *Groundhog Day* since for weeks life seemed to followed a similar sequence. Already semi-conscious, in that foggy noman's land between reality and the terrible nightmare he had just dreamed, he heard the faint, but discernable, metallic click, meaning his beige, Bakelite radio would spring to life with a series of country music songs punctuated by commercials for local businesses, interspersed with today's weather forecast along with some quips regarding upcoming events in the area. Heaving himself out of bed he hurried to the bathroom with, as usual, no time to shower, just enough for a quick shave, after which he dressed and went into the sunlit kitchen, opening the cupboard to grab a small package of Instant Breakfast, which he quickly opened, dissolving it in a glass of milk, which he then chugged down while throwing a quick glance at the wall clock. 6:45 am, right on the old bazoo! He slipped out the front door, making sure to close it firmly behind him, but not too loudly so as not to wake his brother. Five minutes later he drove onto the empty parking lot at the Winn Dixie, satisfied that the others in the car pool hadn't arrived yet. In face of the exploding gas prices, more and more drivers were being forced to re-think their daily modes of transportation, with many, even if grinding their teeth, having to admit that four to a car was far cheaper than one, thus leading to car pools – simple economics. Moreover, the distance to work and back added up to 40 miles a day, five times a week equaled 200 miles flat.

Gradually the other drivers arrived with a curt greeting, parking their vehicles close to another, then meandering over to the designated "driver of the week" to file into his car. Being the youngest and the newest, he dutifully squeezed himself into the back seat beside Mr. Lawton, a teacher, while upfront sat Mr. Hall, office staff plus local preacher, and the driver, a Mr. Lowell, also staff and taught a course on Bible studies too. Just outside the city limits some one brought up the subject of Vietnam, where the North Vietnamese were starting what seemed to be a full-scale offense against the South Vietnamese army up in the northern highlands, with the latter just barely able to hold their positions. While the two men in the front seats were of the opinion that the U.S. should a least offer air support (probably in the back of their minds vaguely remembering the French defeat twenty years ago at Dien Bien Phu), Mr. Lawton renounced any help at all, stating that the U.S. Involvement in Southeast Asia was simply the wrong time, at the wrong place. Being some twenty, twenty-five years younger than those men up in the front seat, Lawton tended to see the war through different lenses than the older ones who distinctly remember WW II and the war in Korea. The other young man in the back seat, not wanting to get involved, kept his mouth shut, closing his eyes as if having drifted off to sleep. One cursory glance at him sufficed to exclude him from the on-going conversation, which, in turn, swiftly concentrated on the results of the present economic recession and its direct effects on their own, immediate lives. Meanwhile, the young man had indeed fallen asleep in the back seat, his head now slumped over against the door, his body held in place by the seat belt. The car, now picking up speed on the short four-lane stretch around Grand Ridge, sped onward toward the Apalachicola River on that chilly January morning in the Florida panhandle.

Great Expectations

After all these years they were once more all together again. After a long drawn out hiatus of some six years, Cliff and Peggy Mann were finally able to corral all five sons together for Christmas at home; their third son's extended sojourn in Berlin plus his fifteen months on Taiwan having finally led to a long-due reunion. Accompanying their Mom to midnight mass at St. Joseph's, the boys came home to a sumptuous meal prepared by their father, which was later followed by a merry exchange of gifts, with Dick, the third son, stealing the show by bestowing each and every brother with a long scroll, on which a Chinese symbol had been carefully calligraphed. Just to add some excitement to the moment, Dick listed all twelve animals of the Chinese zodiac, challenging his brothers to choose the one that they thought was valid for them, promising the winner a six-pack of the beer of their choice. Although they tried their best, all efforts were in vain, because the facts were such – Dave was born in the year of the tiger, Jim was a snake, Doug a monkey and Dan a rat. Dick, himself a horse, made it clear that all the symbols had many positive and negative connotations, with the only real exception being the dragon. After much whiskey, with their Mom pounding out a wide selections of tunes from the Thirties and Forties, the whole family finally decided to hit the hay around 3:30 am. The next morning over brunch, Dick was asked by his parents as to just exactly what he intended to do, now that he was finally back in Florida. Anticipating this very question, he was Johnny-on-the-spot with a convincing answer. Basically his plan was to kill two birds with one stone ; first off he'd use the remaining nine months of his GI Bill to study for three quarters at Florida State, and attain a teaching scholarship while working for his Ph. D. To top things off, he'd then seek out a junior college in Florida and starting teaching there. Any further questions? Of course not, here was a rocket ready for re-launch. His Mom gave him a questioning look, hopeful, but by no means convinced that this would conclude with a happy ending. Dick finished up by adding that he and Jim would be driving up to Tally in two days to put the final touch on things.

However, once in Tallahassee a few days later his confidence quickly started to disintegrate because his visit to the Veteran's Office turned out to be a disaster in that he was bluntly told that his final nine months of GI Bill benefits could only be used on academic work leading to a bachelor's degree. Dick's adamant reply that he had already obtained his BA ,and that his MA from the Free University of West Berlin had been a result of GI Bill benefits from the states failed to cut any ice with the VA office staff, with him being told there was absolutely no chance for him receiving financial aid when working toward a graduate degree. Later that day, he sat down in Jim's house in Marianna, some seventy miles west of the state capital telling his brother his woes, expecting some commiseration, with Jim merely listening stolidly, his mind already seeking alternatives. Seeing that Dick was literally at a dead end, Jim suggested the following plan – until things somehow panned out with the VA, why not start work here in the vicinity so as to fill his empty coffers? Jim would offer him a rent free room if Dick would keep the kitchen clean, buy his own food and do any yard work needed. Reluctantly, with a sense of foreboding, Dick agreed, on the one hand thankful for the gracious offer, but on the other hand, distraught that his future plans which appeared so firm a week ago should now be merely so much spit in the wind.

His best bet seemed to be the Dozier's Boys School just outside of town, which he remembered from his youth, when young boys were, in cases of extremely bad behavior, warned of being "sent up to reform school" in Marianna, a spot so remote, so foreign to their daily lives, that it sent a chill up their backs. No one they ever knew had actually been sent there, but they had heard the scuttlebut that a friend of theirs knew a guy who in turn had heard of a kid, who had been sent up-state to the reform school, where the food was bad and the discipline harsh. Well, it seemed that Jim knew a guy working there, who was willing to find out if there was an opening for a teaching position at the school; and while Dick was not too enthused with the thought of teaching out at Dozier's, at least it would provide him with a job, plus being relatively close to home. Since the application process would take time, Dick was forced to sit around the house, reading and watching TV programs in order to accustom himself to American life-style once again, having been absent some seven long years. Shortly after his arrival in December he had spent the second day watching a full morning of TV shows, both intrigued and appalled by a show entitled *The Newlywed Game* on ABC, where young freshly married couples were competing against one another for prizes. For example, the men were led off-stage, while their spouses were asked by the MC what their husband's favorite vegetable was. Returning to the stage, the men were then asked to name their favorite vegetable. When the answers by the men failed to correspond to those of their wives some of the women were incesenced, screaming that "you always told me that you liked *peas*, not *spinach!*" As the man roared back, "I did *not!* You *know* I always said I actually prefer *corn!*" By now the audience is in stitches, with the MC stoking up the conflict instead of trying to contain it, causing the slanging between the couple to increase in volume, growing in intensity, as the other competing couples offer bemused looks, glad to see the competition self-destruct before an audience beside itself with delight. Dick couldn't believe what he was viewing. Where was the compassion, the empathy needed to help this poor newly wedded couple start to tame their emotions? In fact, neither the MC nor the audience seemed the least bit interested in calming down the conflict, obviously finding a sort of malicious pleasure in watching young newlyweds take each other verbally apart on national television. Flicking off the TV set, Dick wondered if the staff provided any post-show counseling for bitterly disappointed couples, so sure of winning prizes only to be *sabotaged* by a witless partner.

The very next day Jim| told him the bad news; his friend had called him at work, telling him that Dozier's was not interested at the present time, they were having certain "problems", obviously not wanting to go into details; nevertheless, Dick should keep in touch in case of a future job opening. Not wanting to disappoint his brother completely, Jim added a hopeful note in stating that there was a possible job opening over at the state prison close to Chattahoochee and that he'd know by tomorrow if Dick had the necessary credentials for the job. Ugh, Chattahoochee. Why that was close to twenty-five miles away – fifty miles of driving every day. A reform school was bad enough, now a state prison! No, this was not what he had planned for in the past months. He should be at Florida State working on his Ph.D., not teaching at a Florida state prison! Nonetheless, beggars couldn't be choosers, with him financially at the end of his rope, he saw no other immediate alternative than to bite into that sour apple, indeed if it were even offered to him in the first place. One thing was clear, he needed wheels were he to work anywhere, so being kind, Jim offered him a loan in order for Dick to buy a used car; thus he ended up purchasing a baby-blue, six-year old Karmann Ghia, his first automobile ever. Since his drivers license had long expired, he had to take the written test again, this time down at the Blountstown city hall, where he sat perched beside a row of young hayseeds, who came in off the farms and markets, with them giving him the eye and he countering with a supercilious smile. He'd show these panhandle dudes how tests were aced. One hour later he was shocked to hear the the news that he had failed the driver's test, while all four hayseeds had come through with flying colors! There he sat, beaten, chagrined, not able to muster the courage to look the other participants in the face, knowing they were whispering among themselves about what a comeuppance Mr. Smarty Pants had received, as they one by one flashed their new licenses. Grinning broadly, the state official told him he could return next week, and, with a hearty laugh, try his luck again. Struck to the core, Dick literally memorized the manual in the coming days, easily passing the test on his second try.

Running against all expectations, Jim greeted him that evening in early January with a bomb – the administration over at the prison turned out to be desperately seeking a teacher to replace one who was leaving for further studies at a university. Having seen copies of Dick's two degrees, they were anxious to interview him as soon as possible as time was running short, with the teacher planning to leave within the next week. With a somewhat skeptical glance, Jim asked him if he thought he was up to it, teaching in a prison. Not wanting to flinch in front of this brother, Dick attempted to be blasé about the challenge facing him, putting his best foot forward in touting his experience in teaching English at a language school on Taiwan, with his brother quickly interjecting that now he'd be teaching in a *state prison*. Trying his best to remain calm, despite the tremors racing through his mind, he told his brother that he thought he was up to the task, also looking forward to finally earning some cash. Later that night, lying in bed, he began to ruminate on just how his life had suddenly lost its course, one which he had banked upon when returning to the states. His dream of being a teaching assistant at Florida State had been abruptly been replaced by a job teaching inmates at a *much different* state institution on the banks of the Chattahoochee River. So much for his knowledge of German and Chinese, his left-wing political ideas, his optimistic, forward-looking, feeling of *excelsior*! Then, with a deep sigh, he finally was able to drift off to sleep.

Strange New World

E arly that Friday morning saw him speeding along the short, four-lane stretch of highway around Grand Ridge, staring into the glare of the rising sun due east. In his mind he rapidly reviewed his knowledge of general science, particularly chemistry and biology, wanting to be prepared for any questions aimed at him in this area. His original confidence found itself increasingly undermined by the sheer opacity of the process surrounding his hiring, with many steps being simply overleaped by the obvious need for an immediate replacement on the teaching staff. Slowing down a bit, he drove through the sleepy little town of Sneads, having been told that the prison was just a few miles further on the left side of the road. Sure enough, minutes later he spotted the sign – Apalachee Correctional Center, with him swinging his Karmann Ghia into the parking lot, already chock full of cars and pick-up trucks.

Much to his surprise, the large administration building reminded him somewhat of his old high school in Winter Haven with its slow-slung, modern glass and brick, almost campus style look. Greeted effusively by the educational supervisor, Mr. Sexton, a man in his early fifties, he was then quickly ushered into a nearby room to begin the orientation program. So there they sat, the some fifteen persons beginning various jobs at the institution, ranging from maintenance and construction to food service and security, with all candidates seemingly from the local area. Standing out like a sore thumb, Dick tried his best to keep a low profile, swiftly realizing how different he appeared from the others. In his presentation, Mr. Sexton was very low-key, stressing the fact that he too was also from the Panhandle, and also fully aware of the necessity of getting everyone on the same page right from the start. While, on the one hand, he clearly saw all of the departments as equal, Mr. Sexton added that, of course, one area was nevertheless paramount, namely security. This remark received a round of well-meaning laughter since they all knew that security was *the* key department at the institution, or as the supervisor said, "this isn't a Boy Scout camp." Perchance Dick noticed out of the corner of his eye a bright something on the big, beefy hand next to him. Carefully turning his head, not wanting to appear too curious, too invasive, he realized that the object was a ring. Trying his best not to gain the attention of the man beside him, he strained his eyes to his left, now able to decipher the initials surrounding a ruby-red stone atop the ring, *Ku Klux Klan*. Shocked to the core, Dick leaned back in his chair, stunned that this was still possible in the mid-seventies after the civil rights legislation passed by the US Congress in the sixties. During his youth he had heard about the *Klan*, but considered it moribund, a specter of the past, not at all contiguous with the modern South he had envisaged as a student in those turbulent years when Martin Luther King had seized the moral leadership to awaken the US in his struggle against segregation in the south. And now here was Dick sitting beside a member of that organization which was 180° out from his own political convictions. A few minutes later Mr. Saxon had finished his talk, now busy dividing up the group according to their future work places, telling Dick to sit tight, he'd be back in a jiffy to shown him the education tract.

The tract itself was a large, square concrete plaza surrounded by classrooms, all constructed within the last few years. He saw two or three concrete benches on the plaza, otherwise bare of any foliage excepting two small concrete containers housing a few palmettos. Halting before one of the classrooms, Mr. Sexton spoke to Dick quietly, telling him that the science teacher, a certain Mr. Nielson, had received his acceptance at a medical school in New Orleans and would be leaving immediately, with just enough time for Dick to learn the ropes before taking over the reigns on the coming Monday. Then, as an afterthought, the supervisor, almost leaning his head on Dick's shoulder, told him in a firm, distinct tone that he should have his hair cut the next day, seeing as the grooming rules were very strict at ACI – no hair should be touching his ears and, in the back, the hair should be above his collar. Now was that clear? Without the slightest of pauses Dick nodded his head affirmatively.

Although the institution found itself west of the Apalachicola River, clearly in the Central Standard time zone, the prison had decided to use Eastern Standard time since many of the staff came from east of the river, some even making the fifty mile drive all the way from Tallahassee. This meant that in order to arrive on time at 8:00 am at ACI meant leaving Mariana around 6:10 am to be at the institution shortly before 7:00 am, which was, of course, 8:00 am EST. Nonetheless, this had the advantage of being able to leave at 4:00 pm, thus being able to return home shortly before 5:00 pm.

After sharing lunch together, the teacher, Don Nielson, brought Dick over to the empty class room for a jump-start introduction to the teaching program Don had developed in the past months, a system that was as simple as ingenious. He had created a workbook covering all areas of general science from geology to chemistry, from the human body to meteorology, with each chapter being followed by a long, multiple choice test. Thus the students could learn at their own pace, giving the teacher time to aid those students having problems. Amazed at the innate simplicity and efficiency of the program, Dick was quick to praise Don's system which would help him immensely in this transition into a completely new job. As Don busied himself with some last-minute administrative details, Dick began to carefully inspect the room in which he'd be teaching in the coming months.

The long rectangular room had a row of windows facing the plaza, five rows of long, narrow back-topped desks with stools, a large experiment table with water nozzles which also served as a desk, a long, green, chalk-board, a series of big flip charts concerning bone and muscle structures of the human body plus a plastic torso with removable organs. Along with a toilet room, there were two small supply rooms just to the right and left of the green board. Heating and air-conditioning was provided by a long duct running along the ceiling of the right side of the room. For gloomy days there was adequate neon lighting. One had to admit that the teaching conditions were almost optimal, with Dick already alight with ideas of bringing his new students abreast of the important role science played in their everyday lives, and how greater knowledge could lead to further social progress. He could already see the delighted expressions on their faces when they discovered sources of knowledge completely unknown beforehand. Consequently, the motto was now *excelsior*! For his older brother Dave never tired of saying that the most expensive thing you could ever own was your own *ignorance!*

Next Monday morning saw Dick striding across the plaza, his ring of keys jangling from his new key chain up, On entering the classroom some fifteen minutes ahead of the inmates, he quickly ran over the plans for the day, first off trying to deal with the fact that his job consisted of actually teaching two *different* groups each week, with the first group coming on Monday, Tuesday and Wednesday, the second on Thursday and Friday. Then, the next week, the schedule was reversed with first group coming the first two days, the second group the following three. Since he'd be altogether teaching five classes a day, with a one hour break in the afternoon, this meant he'd been teaching a total of ten classes. Glancing down at his class lists he counted an average of some 20-25 persons per class, thus he'd be dealing with roughly some 200 plus inmates per week. Now how in the hell could ever remember all those names?! Especially when the classes changed in the middle of the week! Had he truly bitten off more than he could chew? How could he instill a modicum of discipline if he couldn't get the names straight to begin with? Jesus, his first day on the job and he could feel the first pangs of light panic setting in. The five classes were based on the inmates' educational level from 5 (low) to 1 (high), with those in the latter preparing themselves for the GED (high school equivalency test). Mornings would see him teaching three classes (one for two hours) with a long lunch break, followed by two more classes with a one hour pause between them, Dick's "free time", so to speak.

Shortly after 8:00 am he heard a low, muffled roar. Darting to the window he saw a blue wave of inmates streaming across the plaza heading for the classrooms and, sure enough, seconds later the door to the room burst open to a flood of bodies all dressed in their light-blue uniforms, jostling one another, prattling loudly, with merely a cursory glance at their new teacher. Waiting for things to calm down, Dick played for time by studying the list of names lying on his desk, before beginning the daunting process of trying to match each name to a particular person. So, biting into the sour apple, he started to go down the list alphabetically, receiving different responses, some slightly hostile in tone, others more friendly, some decidedly neutral, with Dick having trouble memorizing names and faces, hardly able to remember a quarter of his class after the first rôle call. But what now, how best to introduce himself to this phalanx of blue sitting impatiently in front of him? Sensing that the time had come for a clear reaction on his part, Dick strolled over to the row of windows and, leaning back, turned to the inmates, nervously beginning what he hoped would be a convincing talk concerning his future expectations of how he would be teaching the class.

"First off, let me say that I'm pleased to be following Mr. Nielson, who has done such a great job in creating a system whereby each student can work at his own pace, thus providing me with time to check your work, offer tips and correct the tests taken at the end of each chapter. As far as I'm concerned, each of you has a clean slate, I'll do my best to treat you as fairly as possible. After looking through the texts you'll be reading, I think all of you, if you work hard, can end up taking the GED test, thus receiving a high school diploma." It was here that he heard the first snickers of disbelief.

"Now I know that some of you may not think you're capable of this...but I am convinced that you can. Think of each class as an escalator, constantly moving upward toward a goal, the GED. If we work together as team, we can achieve this goal."

In the background there were snorts of laughter.

"Some you may not yet possess the knowledge necessary. *Not yet*. However, in the coming months we'll tackle all the problems you have with the course contents, with some of you being surprised at your own abilities. Why, once you've advanced from the lower levels up to the 4th and 5th, I intend to have you doing *experiments* right in our own classroom."

Looking at the incredulous faces in front of him, plastered with grins of doubt, Dick impetuously decided to up the ante.

"I can see that some of you think this is impossible, right? Well, I've got news for you – *it's not!* Sure it's a long row to hoe, but if you put your mind to the task, your shoulder to the wheel, why we could, in the future, be learning at a *junior college level!"*

The spontaneous outburst of laughter was loud and long, with Dick finally just starting to grasp the true reality of his situation, as he trod back to his desk up front, passing out the workbooks to the inmates, now abashed that he had even dared mention the words *junior college*. Where was his mind, what was he thinking of?! Quickly scanning the unrest in the classroom, it became crystal clear to him that he'd had enough of a problem with classroom discipline. Well, maybe these were difficulties of a beginner, surely things would improve as time went on and the class would soon come to realize the truth, the fact that they had a teacher who was convinced that they were victims of the capitalist system (rich vs. poor), not to mention the racism, particularly prevalent in the Deep South. Time and patience would suffice; through his own attitude and hard work he would make it abundantly clear that he was here to *help* them if they'd just give him a proper chance.

By the time lunch rolled around he was starving - just that one glass of *Instant Breakfast* to tide him over until 12:30! Actually the cafeteria was a complete *novum* to him, where inmates brought each staff member a meal to the table. Not only that, much of the food was raised right on the prison grounds! Finicky in his youth regarding food, Dick now found himself scarfing down vegetables he wouldn't have touched as a teenager. Squash, okra, collard greens went right down the hatch, as he kept a low profile at the table, surrounded by staff members engrossed in their own world, with him all ears, just trying to grasp the names, decode the many abstruse statements flying by. After lunch he retired to his classroom, resting his head on the desk, closing his eyes, trying his best to catch forty winks before the next class arrived.

As the car headed west along highway 90 into a setting winter sun, Dick sat scrunched up in the rear seat lost in his own thoughts, barely able to follow the flow of conversation around him. He had managed to eak out a victory of sorts with the two classes taught after lunch, not having met with enthusiasm, but no outright hostility. He kept reviewing some of the pertinent facts learned on the job. First off, he found out that he was working on the so-called "high side" i.e., with those inmates thought capable, over time, of acquiring enough information as to successfully pass the GED test ; the "low side" being made for those young men who were categorized as being "slow learners" or "academic stragglers", most merely possessing basic primary school skills, having major problems in reading, writing and doing math. On the average Dick had estimated that his white students made up some 40% of his classes, while some 45% were black, the other 5% hispanic. However, the 1st level was around 65% black, while the 5th consisted of approximately 70% whites. It seemed to him that the majority of the whites more or less accepted him in good stead as their teacher, the blacks, on the other hand, appeared more reluctant in their support, probably more cautious in general as to if this newly-minted young white teacher from afar could really push his agenda through, with some tough inmates seemingly ready and willing to test his mettle.

That same evening over supper, he described in detail the events of the day to his curious brother who displayed real sympathy, telling Dick he'd keep his fingers crossed for him in the coming weeks, adding that he was throwing his yearly "pig roast" in about two weeks, with a whole passle of friends coming over to the house on a Saturday afternoon. Now that sufficed to brighten Dick's visage accordingly. Afterward he cleaned up the dishes, then headed into his room to finish giving it the final touch, making it his room. A long, wooden door supported by four concrete blocks on each end served as spacious desk. On the wall to his right was a black and white photo of Salvadore Allende over which stood a smaller orange and white poster from the *Jungsozialisten* in the SPD. Down below, the *Bali Kino* in Berlin announced it was showing the the film *Kuhle Wampe* from the early 1930's. Over to his left there was a caricature drawn by Daumier. Astride the desk stood his faithful Grundig Satellite radio next to a pile of papers and an old, battered Chinese-German dictionary, all moot tribute to two worlds light-years away from where he was now, out in the middle of the Florida panhandle with Tallahassee to east, Panama City on the Gulf coast and Dothan, Alabama up to the northwest. Hot damn, was he ever down south now!

Much too occupied the first week with trying to get a handle on his classes, particularly in his failing attempt to associate names with faces, by the second week he was also gradually becoming aware of the other teachers and their influence on the inmates. The math teacher, a big, sturdy woman named Mrs. Ball reminded him of his 3rd grade teacher, Mrs. Arrington, only bigger, tougher. When meeting her for the first time, she kept her distance from him, not unfriendly, but rather cool. Dick could tell which teacher the inmates had had as soon as they arrived in his classroom. When they came from math class they were mostly quiet, almost as if they had been to a certain degree emasculated in the last hour. However, when they came from next door, Mr. Hargreave's room, they were loose and a bit yancy, since their English teacher was *not* a stickler for discipline, thus meaning that Dick too, would have to deal with the after-effects of this liberal climate for the following hour. Mrs. Allen, a pleasant young woman in her early thirties the next room down, taught health, seemed to have discovered some secret method of instilling respect in her students, for when Dick happened to visit her one door down, her class was quiet and worklike. Around the corner, catty-corner from Dick's own room, Mr. Spikes, the social studies teacher appeared to be locked in combat with the inmates, with Dick sensing a rather intense dislike of one for the other on both sides. Spikes was a local, actually a farmer who sort of taught on the side to make ends meet, as the teacher's salaries were anything but high paying. Dick's own starting salary as a Classroom II teacher amounted to a paltry $11,000 a year. Why fifteen years ago that kind of money almost made you upper middle-class. Back in Winter Haven in 1960 ,Mr. Sonderlundt with a Ph.D in chemistry was earning $250 a week out at the Bird's Eye plant. If Dick were married with two kids and a wife at home they'd be a poverty case, having to sign up for food stamps! As he saw it, the fifties and sixties were history; now one had to have a high salary or have the wife working too in order to support a nuclear family of four – what massive socio-economic changes had taken place in such a short period of time.

Friday afternoon found him crossing the Apalachicola River, driving through Chattahoochee heading for Tallahassee for the weekend. His brother Doug and wife Karen lived there in a medium-sized bungalow style house with a roomy garden in the back. Doug, after graduating from FSU, found employment at the state retirement department, with an adequate salary, a rather large office and secretary. All in all he should have been satisfied, but suffered under a growing feeling of being somewhat *underemployed*, his duties being mostly of a mundane nature, his boss telling the staff that the most important goal was for them *not to make waves*, thus any changes which might provoke the slightest political unrest remained in abeyance, only spoken about privatly, never brought to print or suggested at meetings. One of Dick's co-workers at ACI, a certain young man his age, Mr. Lawton, had warned him early on to be careful of what he said around other staff members. Lawton's motto: "*Don't spill the beans.*"

Just outside of Tally the *Blaupunkt* radio blurted out the surprising news that one of the original *Three Stooges*, Larry Fine, had died that very day in Los Angeles at the age of 74. Oh, no, not Larry. He had always been a favorite of Dick's, who considered Moe to be too brutal, Shemp a bit dense, with Larry being somewhere in between, one could say, perhaps more sympathetic. At any rate he was saddened by the news, remembering all those Saturday afternoons at the Grand Theater in his home town, where the kids went to see cowboy movies, serials, a cartoon… and, of course, the *Three Stooges*. Moreover, this sudden jolt forced upon him the unpleasant thought that he'd turn 33 this coming summer; 33 with no wife (not even a girlfriend), no kids and no inkling as to where life was taking him, his optimistic plans of the past years now lying in shreds, with him not being able to come up with a viable alternative to his present life, feeling himself increasingly being more and more a passive observer of events around him, moved by forces beyond his control.

Doug and his wife Karen, who taught marriage counseling over at Florida A&M, had other plans for the evening, so after a tasty meal they dropped Dick off at the FSU campus where he was set to meet with his youngest brother Dan and his fiancée, who possessed tickets for a talk by Dan Rather, an up and coming correspondent of CBS news. This occurred quite often on US college campuses, with a wide spectrum of speakers invited during the semester to give talks to the students on a variety of subject. Remembering well the brief meeting in the spring of 1966 with Henry Kissinger, then a professor at Harvard, Dick looked forward to an entertaining evening in the student auditorium. Dan and Betty had arrived in advance, reserving him a seat, greeting him cordially, asking him if his work over at ACI was on the road to success, with Dick replying, hoping to avoid any in-depth discussion, that, to be truthful, it was simply too early to tell. Luckily for Dick, the lights dimmed a bit as a member of the student government read a short CV of Dan Rather's life before the man himself entered the stage to friendly applause.

From the start one could definitely see that Dan was used to such a public environment, at ease in front of the audience, armed with a bevy of humorous quips delivered in a lightly self-depreciating manner, well-suited to the youthful visitors, who seemed to take an instant liking to this trim, tanned young man, with a slight, but noticeable, southern accent. Without further ado, Dan asked the audience if they were aware of what important event was taking place right now in Washington, the nation's capital? As the silence grew, he answered the question himself, stating that the presidential campaign for the Fall elections in 1976 *had already started*! Wow, now that really caught everybody off guard. Quickly he followed this up by stating that while campaign contributions were limited in Congressional elections, at the present there were *no limitations* on contributions to presidential candidates, and thus possible future candidates were already out on the hustings, hoping to begin filling up their rather meager war-chests by wealthy supporters. During the one hour talk, filled with pertinent facts and critical arguments, while never demanding new legislation limiting such contributions, he made it perfectly clear that the students should *wake up* and *become aware* of what was transpiring beyond the borders of their own campus. They should *be concerned* over those powerful, economic forces working *behind the scenes*, exerting an inexorable influence on the upcoming elections next year. Following a rather mundane question and answer routine after the end of the talk, the students gave the visitors a long, generous round of applause, before filing back to their dorms, or in the case of Dick, Dan and Betty, opting for a few beers before heading home. Both enthusiastic over the contents of the talk, Dick and Dan were amazed to hear Betty dryly opine that the extemporaneous speech by Dan Rather, by no means trivial, actually bordered somewhat on the commonplace. Adding insult to injury, she added that, in a way, well, he was really no better than a one-trick pony, seizing on one theme and riding it until it was exhausted. Pausing to take another sip of beer, the men were more or less forced to agree with her, Dick having listened to all sorts of arcane talks by guest speakers while a student in Gainesville, one of whom was convinced that life existed on Mars. And to think that that man was *paid* big bucks for his talk!

Spring Tide Rising

By the early spring of 1975 the effects of the growing economic recession in the US, having begun by the Arab oil embargo some eighteen months before, then further exacerbated by Washington's fiscal policy, had resulted in a major increase in the number of inmates being funneled into the state's prison system, straining their capacities to the utmost, with subsequent tension, due to severe overcrowding. During lunch the other teachers were beginning to complain about their classes being stuffed full, leaving them unable to aid those inmates needing their help. Of course these conditions also led to a rise in the general level of disciplinary problems, with teachers sacrificing precious class time just to keep a lid on some of the more recalcitrant inmates.

In his own classroom Dick had his own hands full trying to keep control of the classes, many of which were first being subtly sabotaged, then more blatantly by a small handful of inmates, passing notes to one another, interrupting his conversations, firing spit-balls at him or whistling in a low tone, making it almost impossible to correctly identify the culprit. He found, much to his dismay, that his level 5 class, after the GED test had reduced the number from some 25 down to 11 or 12, was stocked back up with new inmates within three or four days. Now this ticked him off because he found that 12 was the optimal number of inmates; of course when the administration quickly began filling up his level 5 class with new inmates this didn't initially hinder his teaching since there really wasn't such a big difference between 12 and, say 15. However, when they continued to ratchet up the numbers to 16, then 17 and beyond, all the noticeable advantages of lesser numbers swiftly disappeared, so within ten days his class was once again just as large as all the others. Consequently the rising pressure on the whole institution was mirrored within Dick's own classroom – a microcosm of it all, with him teeter-tottering on the brink.

Alleviating his dour mood somewhat, Jim, aware of his brother's situation, gently coaxed him into working with him to help stage the annual "pig roast" in the back yard. Jim had chosen to invite around sixty old friends and acquaintances over to his house on a Saturday afternoon for a party which would last late into the evening. Friday evening Jim and Dick went shopping over at Winn-Dixie for the upcoming backyard picnic, loading up particularly with many a case of beer since most of the invitees were young men. The next morning saw them assiduously setting up tables and chairs in the backyard, after which they began excavating a long trench in the lawn, some five feet long, three feet wide, around 18 inches deep, to hold all the charcoal. Jim's friend, Bruce, would arrive shortly, driving over from Cottondale to set up the spit, being very experienced with roasting pigs. Driving over to a local 7:11 store, Dick purchased several sacks of crushed ice for the beer and soft drinks, while Jim and another friend worked on setting up a small salad bar. By noon they had finished their work, stopping for a bite to eat, while awaiting the arrival of the first guests.

By three o'clock the house and lawn were chock-a-block with a mixture of friends from everywhere – locals from Marianna and thereabouts, Jackson county, Panama City and quite a few having driven over from Tallahassee, Jim's old stomping grounds. In the living room a group of younger men were scrunched around a TV console, where they were trying out a brand-new video game called *Pong*, a kind of table tennis game, in which two contestants tried to judge the movements of a ping-pong ball crossing the console screen, each possessing a racquet so they could send the ball back toward their opponent. The game demanded a modicum of eye-hand coordination, which, in turn, was partially determined by the player's skill, but also how much beer he had consumed by then. Tired of waiting for his turn to play the new game, Dick wandered over to the middle of the living room where five or six young men were standing around, a beer can in one hand, the other free for gestures in their intensive conversation. As he approached the group he was amazed at the sheer size of the guys, hell, they must have all been around six foot three or four, long and lanky, alongside them Jim (just a tad under six feet) appeared rather small, whereas Dick, well, beside the rest of them he seemed somehow foreshortened, truncated, a young boy lost in the valley of the giants. Before he could begin to fall into that spiral of doubt and despair which he knew from his years as a young teenager, he felt someone tug on his shoulder and, pivoting around he recognized Pete Pederson, one of Jim's younger friends. Pete was on a spring break from Southern Mississippi College down in Hattiesburg, the same town from where one of Dick's old Navy buddies had hailed from – a nice guy, but much too "old South" for Dick's critical eye. With gusto Pete picked up on just this theme, making fun of those "good old boys" on campus, who still had confederate flags in their rooms, were politically extremely conservative, and still clinging to the norms and folkways of the 1950's. In particular he lashed out at the young ladies at the school, their exaggerated decorum and lack of intellectual curiosity, damning them as a bunch of "magnolias", saying this was the pejorative term used on campus. Pete ended his tirade by stating that he was looking forward to returning to Tallahassee as soon as possible.

Late that same evening, long after everyone had departed, Jim and Dick, tired from the strenuous clean-up action following the roast, sat in the living room sipping their beers, letting the whole day slowly pass in review. Having played a rather minor role in the whole shindig, Dick was nevertheless in full praise of his brother for having organized such a successful social event, where all participants lauded Jim for such an outstanding pig roast. However, he was slightly disconcerted to see his

His brother so quiet, so pensive. Then, hesitantly, Jim began with a critical assessment of the whole afternoon and evening, coming to the conclusion that the game wasn't worth the candle, so to speak. Astonished at this, Dick queried his brother as to how he managed to arrive at such a negative conclusion, when literally *all* of his friends were more than satisfied? Leaning back in his chair Jim sighed, his following plaintive words almost tumbling out in jumbles. No, this type of pig roast party was definitely *not* what he had intended at the beginning, however, the thing had been transformed, diverting it from his original goal. The whole idea was to meet with old and new friends on a long afternoon of food, drink and conversation, but now, due to growing size of the fest, Jim had found himself scampering around the house and yard and, despite Dick's and Bruce's aid, trying his best to make sure all was running as planned, not able to find the time to sit down and reminisce with his buddies, these futile attempts constantly interrupted by those seeking some arcane information regarding social security or complaining about the lack of a certain food or last year's football season or some other godforsaken theme which had popped up into the intruder's mind while munching on the crisp roast pig. To top things off, Jim added caustically, he himself found the whole shebang becoming more expensive every year! No, the whole thing had gotten out of hand and he was seriously thinking of cancelling the idea of throwing another party in 1976. Either that or strictly reduce the number of guests. With a gesture of disgust Jim marched off into the bedroom, seeking solace and sleep, leaving Dick alone in the living room to ruminate on the day's events. He had to think of the quote from *Winnie the Pooh* which went like this: "I don't see much sense in that," said Rabbit. "No, said Pooh humbly, there isn't." "But there was when I began it, it's just that something happened to it along the way."

A week later, and unexpected guest arrived in Marianna, having hours beforehand announced his coming via a brief telephone call from Pensacola. Dick's old friend, Al Soderlundt, was planning to drop by for a quick visit, before moseying on down-state, wanting to know if Jim could put them up for the night. Not particularly surprised, knowing Al, Jim agreed to make a place in the living room, for Al would also be coming with wife and infant. Both brothers were interested in seeing their friend, whom they hadn't seen *in a coon's age*.

That evening Jim cooked up some scrumptious chili con carne without the least forethought in mind, only to discover that Al's wife, Julie, was a 100% vegetarian, with the cook swiftly managing to offer some scrambled eggs as compensation. Later, over some beer and wine, Al slowly began explaining the reasons behind his sudden appearance in Florida, since, having been born and raised in California, Al had always stated that he would some day end up way out West, in this case, Colorado. The last few years had seen him living in a hippie community out in the Rocky Mountains, where life was spartan, but simple, with few hassles. Bob Seward, after his six-month sojourn in Europe, which ended with the US government paying for his flight back to the states, Bob having become paranoid in the last years through his indiscriminate use of drugs – Dick having experienced this directly when Bob had, unannounced, suddenly showed up at *Haus 16* in the *Studentendorf Schlachtensee* in June,1970. At present, however, according to Al, Bob was off the hard drugs, merely smoking lots of grass and popping tranquilizers, trying to maintain a precarious balance.

Perhaps a bit impatiently, Jim queried him as to exactly why he had now decided to move back to Florida. Al answered that he and Julie had been living in some previously uninhabited pueblo dwellings, close to a large hispanic settlement. Well, it seems as if, for some reason completely unknown to Al, some of the locals had taken umbrage of these *Anglos* living next to them, telling them they didn't belong in the area and to *vamos*! When Al, cool as ever, ignored these warnings, the

Hispanics took things into their own hands. Thus late one evening, two pickup trucks came roaring up to Al's pueblo hut, tossing fire-bombs at it, all the while taking pot-shots at the hut. That sufficed, with Al and Julie (now lumbered with an infant) thinking wisdom the better part of valor, and they quickly decided to pack up and leave for Florida. Al mentioned having some land east of Gainesville in view, him still in contact with some of his friends from the sixties, who were living in the area. The very next day they left for Winter Haven, intending to visit Al's parents down there before making any major decisions.

Spring had come a little early that year, thus the mild weather found Dick sitting out on the steps of the education compound facing due south, enjoying the lunch break to the fullest, reading an article from the German weekly newspaper *Die Zeit*, which printed an edition in Canada. A slightly shortened edition to be true, but nonetheless one way to keep him informed about events in the country where he had spent over five important years of his life. He was deeply engrossed in the newspaper when he noticed a shadow darkening the newspaper. Looking up saw Ellen Sue, one of the young office secretaries he had briefly seen talking to other teachers, a dark-blonde girl in her early twenties. Not wanting to appear snobby, he lowered the newspaper, greeting her cordially, as she sat down beside him, asking him just what kind of newspaper was he reading? That proved to be the start of a short, lively conversation in which Ellen Sue quickly took the lead, be-laboring him with questions about how he ended up at ACI, how come he had studied both in Gainesville *and* Berlin and finally, as a kind of ad lib remark, were any of his inmates attending the Bible courses? Now this really blindsided him, Bible courses? Never heard of them. Well, she sure had, and off she went on a long tagent, speaking in glowing terms about the classes taught by a lay-preacher, out of Marianna! Of course these classes were voluntary, inmates free to chose for them-selves, however, Ellen Sue was cocksure that those taking the courses would be unlikely to be recidivists, many having renounced their former life of sin, ready to accept Jesus Christ as their savior. As the 1:00 pm bell rang ending the lunch break, she suddenly reached into her handbag, placing a small booklet, a sort of religious tract into Dick's hand before he could say Jack Robinson.

That evening, alone at his desk, he started perusing the little tract he had been so furtively given during the lunch break. The small booklet was about 3 x 2 inches and was entitled "Holy Joe". In just a few minutes Dick was able to gain the gist of the story, a tale he found amusing, but one he thought could be effective on certain souls. The story went more or less like this: A true believer had been drafted into the army, and was derided, hassled endlessly by his top sergeant especially in the form of all the dirty jobs, like doing KP for example. However, instead of giving in or going on a rant, "Holy Joe", as he was called, joyfully sang religious hymns as he washed the pots and pans, chirping that "there was room at the cross for you". Thereupon the sergeant sent him to the base psychiatrist, who was shocked by the brashness of the young soldier telling him straight to his face - "look at *you* sir, miserable, lost, without hope, full of frustrations and *going to hell!*" After having kicked the young man out of his office, the shrink was shaken by the after thought - "Good grief, what if what that kid said was *true?*" Some months later when the unit found itself in combat with the Viet Cong deep in the Vietnamese mountains, a man was needed for an extremely dangerous reconnaissance mission with the sergeant, tossing a gleeful glance at corporal Henderson (who also had cursed at "Holy Joe" for his constant proselytizing) adding, "I know just the man for this mission!" When "Holy Joe" fails to return, the sergeant and Henderson go looking for him, finding his dead body in a small clearing. The sergeant, now suddenly filled with true remorse, sinks down beside the corpse, begging forgiveness for his present and past sins. His repentance is interrupted by Cpl. Henderson screaming, "It's a trap, we're surrounded, run for it Sarg!", before being cut down by enemy fire, a fate which awaits the sergeant too. Later, at the Final Judgment, the sergeant receives a last minute reprieve because of his acknowledgement of Jesus Christ and is consequently saved. Henderson, however, the non-believer, is sent directly to hades. Fondling the tract in his hand, Dick decided to let sleeping dogs lie by simply stashing it into his briefcase, not wanting to pursue the subject any further, figuring that if he just let the matter ride it would soon be forgotten. But, much to his chagrin, it was not.

Hardly had a week passed by when, once again, Ellen Sue caught him out on the steps filching a bit of sun during the lunch break. Without further ado, she broached the subject of the religious tract, asking Dick directly if he had read it and what he thought of it, thus ensuing the following conversation:

Dick (guardedly): "Well, yeah, I read it."

Ellen Sue (curious): "And? What did you think of it?"

Dick (slowly): "...er, I found it i n t e r e s t i n g, perhaps a bit simplistic."

Ellen Sue (with a frown): "So, what was simplistic about it? The message was clear and true, can't you see that?"

Dick (honestly): "Sure. I just don't thinking one should go around proselytizing, you know, kind of selling religion. Do you think that's right, to go around preaching to other people, other cultures?"

Ellen Sue (firmly): "It's not only right, it's our *duty!*"

Dick (taken aback): "Duty? It's your *duty?*"

Ellen Sue: "Sure, it's an obligation to save as many souls as possible, both here in the US and abroad. That's why one of my relatives was a missionary in Africa for three years. Now don't you think that's a wonderful thing, aiding the poor natives and also saving their souls?"

Dick: "Well, I'm glad to hear that somebody in your family was out helping people in the Third World since they certainly need all the help they can get. On the other hand, however, I don't think it's wise to be *selling* our religion to foreign cultures – they have their *own* beliefs and values."

Ellen Sue (emphatically): "But it's our Christian duty to save their souls!"

Dick: "Now how do you figure that? Why should we be telling them what to believe?"

Ellen Sue (gravely): "Because if we don't, they'll end up burning in hell."

Dick: "Now Ellen Sue, tell me how you come to *that* conclusion."

Ellen Sue: "Very simple. If you don't believe in Jesus Christ as your savior, well you won't be saved on judgement day."

Dick (shaking his head): "No, no, that doesn't make sense. What about those poor natives out in the boondocks who have never heard of Jesus, people who are illiterate, who don't possess radios, but are hardworking, decent human beings?"

Ellen Sue (triumphantly): "Exactly. That's the whole point. Missionaries are out there saving those souls who would otherwise end up going to hell. Now, you tell me me, isn't that a worthy task?"

Dick (dazed): "You mean to tell me that people who have never had the slightest chance of ever hearing about Jesus Christ are doomed to burn in hell?"

Ellen Sue: "Yes, because if you don't believe, you can't go to heaven."

Dick (testily): "But where's the Christian compassion for other humans! With this judgment, you're condemning *innocent people* to a horrible fate without giving them the slightest chance to save themselves!"

Ellen Sue: "Well, that's why we need more missionaries. Can't you see this?"

Dick: "But where do you get this idea that people who don't believe in Jesus will all end up in hell? It all sounds so harsh, almost vindictive."

Ellen Sue (sadly): "Yes, I know. Besides, you never can tell when the devil will appear or what form he will take. Leading a true Christian life is a real struggle, let me tell you, but luckily, here at ACI we have a lot of concerned Christians, who…"

Looking down at his wrist-watch Dick saw it was just about time for class to start, so he jumped up, interrupting Ellen Sue with a parting question.

Dick: "So you're saying that if one doesn't believe in Jesus he's doomed to rot in hell forever, right?"

Ellen Sue: "That's correct."

Dick: "And how do you know this?"

Ellen Sue (smiling): "Because it says so *in the Bible.*"

Despite all of his well-intentioned efforts, his attempts at finding a modus vivendi with the inmates were torpedoed again and again by malevolent acts deliberately aimed at disturbing his teaching; these small, niggling acts, while none of which per se were terribly grave, still possessed, however, just enough attention so as to keep a steady state of tension in the classroom, negating to a certain extent, his vision of leading his students on to a higher plane, a more relaxed atmosphere, in which they'd be able to concentrate more effectively. Instead, they (not all, but some) were instigating against him, derisively laughing at him when he forgot their names – hell, how could he remember over 240 names in a few weeks! -, taking organs from the torso model, leaving them scattered all over the room, trying to steal the answer sheets to chapter tests, occasionally firing spit balls at him from the back rows, crossing their arms and lying their heads down going to sleep, fiddling around with the water spigots on his table desk, these and countless other shenanigans which kept him in a constant state of nervousness, not knowing what to expect next, thus unable to relax, always tense, awaiting the brazen act from the seemingly incorrigible inmates. Even worse, this tension carried over into his private life with him becoming more cantankerous around the house, often withdrawing into his room, deliberately reducing his contact to his brother to an absolute minimum. Moreover, he began suffering from nightmares, all having to do with the mutinous class behavior experienced during the day. My God was he ever becoming bitter! He, who always had the best interests of his students in mind, he with his multitude of international experience at hand, he who was always ready to extend his hand, ready to begin a dialog, talk things over, reach a viable compromise, be fair and transparent in his decisions; he who, in the worst case, would just kick the can further down the road, discovered much to his chagrin, that the road was coming to a swift end. Things could not continue like this – something must be done.

The next evening when he opened his copy of *Die Zeit* he was shocked to learn that the CDU candidate for the upcoming election in West Berlin had been kidnapped by a so-called *Bewegung 2. Juni* and held prisoner. He was later released unharmed after other members of the terrorist group were freed. This *Untat* was exactly what his girl friend, Hildegard, had warmed against back in 1972, with him agreeing whole heartedly that terrorism would end in a political dead-end. Neverthe-less he found himself fondly reminiscing of those halcyon days as a student at the *Otto-Suhr-Institut* when he was convinced that there was a glowing future in store for him and friends… only to end up in this cesspool of a prison, where the inmates, who should be shouting hosanna that they were blessed with such a teacher, were intransigent, if not openly hostile to all his efforts in improving their knowledge of science – which was why homo sapiens no longer lived in caves. If they had only been taught the immanent importance of natural science! Their ignorance was often mind boggling! Why just the other day one of his students had come up to him after class, posing an unusual ques-tion to him. Many of the black inmates had scoffed at him when he said that men had landed on the moon, maintaining that it was a hoax, hav-ing taken place in a TV studio. Well, this particular young, black in-mate, told him that, yes, he believed that man had successfully landed on the moon; however, his question was why didn't they fall off? Dick had great difficultly in understanding exactly what he meant. Fall off? How could one fall off the moon? After a series of questions, Dick was able to grasp the essence of what the young man was thinking. He thought that the moon was about the size of Manhattan and hovered about some twenty miles or so above the earth. Thus the inmate was astounded to learn that the moon was around a quarter the size of the earth and some 250.000 miles away. The more he considered this, the more riled up Dick became. He was sick and tired of these goddamned recalcitrant inmates, these ignorant sons-of-bitches, harassing his ass. No, goddamn it, he was going to turn the tables on them, teach them a lesson by harassing *their* young asses! Starting next week he would hard-ass them at the slightest infraction, having already a vicarious pleasure in thinking up forms of punishment to fit the crimes. Topping off everything was the absolute conviction of doing *the right thing*, creating, admittedly through brachial methods, a classroom climate suitable for learning. Undoubtedly it would be a Herculean task, but one which could no longer be procrastinated. Realizing he'd have to do this alone, by himself, he began steeling himself in advance for the coming conflict, knowing that this 180° course change would illicit a tremendous blow-back of resistance from many of the inmates. That night he slept peacefully, probably caused by the deep satisfaction of having finally crossed the Rubicon and would soon be starting to burn the bridges behind him.

That weekend Dick stayed home in Marianna instead of, as so often, driving over to Tallahassee since Jim and Pete Pederson had left for a brief camping expedition in the Appalachians, somewhere close to the Georgia-North Carolina border. Both had been talking the trip up for a while now and, despite the fact that spring still hadn't sprung, they were froggy to hit the road. In the meantime Dick had been invited over by the neighbors, an older married couple which lived across the street, so Saturday afternoon he dressed up a little (but not *too* much), spending the next ninety minutes drinking coffee, eating doughnuts, while chatting rather aimlessly with the couple, knowing full well which subjects were third rail, ambidextrously side-stepping an attempt to get anyway near politics or religion, keeping the conversation as bland as butter, occasionally waving the flag (but not *too* much), revving up his southern accent a bit so as to show that, he too, was a native Floridian. Jim had already told him to be extra nice to the couple since in the past they had always kept an eye out on his house whenever he was gone, a kind of free insurance if you may. In order to keep the conversation rolling, Dick inadvertently posed a simple pro forma question about the town's history, causing the couple to roll their eyes in disbelief. Hadn't anyone yet told him of the famous "Battle of Marianna" during the Civil War? Incredulous at their neighbor's ignorance regarding local history, they avidly filled him in on all the details of the battle in the fall of 1864, where superior Yankee forces had defeated an ad-hoc Confederate group of old men and young boys, ending up with the Episcopal church being set on fire, with many Confederate *still inside*! Fittingly, this was referred to as "Florida's Alamo". Moreover, in keeping with the importance of this events, there was an historical reenactment every year in downtown Marianna, now how about that! Dick answered honestly that, as a newling, he realized how little he knew regarding the lay of the land in Jackson county. Thanking the pair for the coffee and doughnuts, he returned home, spending the greater part of the evening writing a letter to a girl friend on Taiwan, doing his level best to work on expanding his Chinese vocabulary plus exercise his skill in writing Chinese characters. Of course, he avoided any details of his present job, which would be hard to explain in Chinese and lower his stock still further, him stuck out here in the Florida panhandle, lost in the Bermuda triangle between Tally, Panama City and Dothan, Alabama, with him experiencing a wholly new life-style, seeing things he'd never seen before. Why just yesterday he had been out at the Winn Dixie store shopping for some groceries and, while standing in line at the cashier's, had seen a man buying all sorts of unhealthy food: popsicles, candy, cola, sugary cereals, bacon, eggs, fatty meats – all heavy duty. Even more amazing was the fact that the man, who seemed so normal, middle-class, paid the bill with *food stamps!* Dick had *heard* of food stamps, but never seen them. Was this a scam of some sorts or was the man really so poor? Unsure of a convincing answer, Dick simply stored this away in the back of his mind, unable to come to a final conclusion. Late Sunday afternoon Jim returned home, with Dick curious as to what had caused him and Pete to cancel their mountain hike, suspecting that it had something to do with the unexpected cold front which had dropped down from Canada on the weekend. That night over a hot meal Jim told in detail his via dolorosa, particularly Saturday night when the temperature had dropped below freezing with heavy snowfall setting in along with a stinging wind. Both were starting to get the chilly-willys, with Jim even imagining just running out of the tent and down the hill, anything, anywhere, just get away and head home!

Class *War*: *Wipeout All Resistance*

I n the warm, moist early spring morning air the car sped along highway 90 into a cascade of glaring sunlight which proffered another hot, sticky day ahead for those Monday morning riders. Ensconced in the back seat as usual he began rather nervously running through just how he would break the news to the class within the next hour, realizing that this was *the moment*, it was fish or cut bait, and, feeling himself literally at the end of his rope, he knew he had to *stand tall* today – or everything would be to no avail. Then, right in the middle of a discussion up front over the gas prices, the radio, which had been kept down to a low tone, was turned up so as to hear the 6:30 news. A hush suddenly reigned up front as the announcer spoke in a grave voice about the north Vietnamese army having launched an offensive in the central mountains, with the south Vietnamese trying their best to tenaciously hold on, but being forced to slowly retreat. Vietnam again. Ever since the US withdrew its last infantry units in 1972, the South Vietnam government had had its hands full trying to cope with the pressure from the local Vietcong forces and the much more powerful army, with Hanoi gradually gaining the upper hand. A decade since the US marines landed on the coast around DaNang, Americans had become accustomed to receiving *bad news* from Indochina, millions of dollars down the drain, thousands of soldiers dead and wounded, to what end? Consequently, the latest news cast a visible pall over the car, halting the conversation, with the listeners sitting stone-faced in their seats, looking silently as Grand Ridge flew by. When the small talk resumed, it was at a lower tone, almost as if the news from southeast Asia had dampened temporarily spirits of the riders.

The weekend had been spent repeatedly going over the list of names, so he more or less knew in advance who was absent, without having to embarrass himself by calling out names, thus he was immediately able to get down to brass tacks. With a grim visage he told the inmates that he was sick and tired of *taking shit* from them. New rules were being promulgated here now and these included:

- Inmates were to ask permission to use the toilet.
- Inmates were *not* to talk with one another during class – unless permitted by the teacher.
- There was to be no eating of any kind.
- Work books were not to be mistreated – written on, dog-eared, etc.
- If an inmate needed help or wanted to pose a question, he must raise his hand.
- Inmates were not allow to switch seats.
- In regard to infractions, a "three-strike rule" was to be instituted, meaning that the third check by a students name meant he would be immediately be sent to the front office, facing disciplinary measures.

Grim faced, he asked his transfixed listeners if they had understood him? A sea of dumbfounded inmates nodded silently in agreement. Actually he had more or less expected this reaction since this was one of his better classes in regard to comportment – the real test lay not only in one or two classes. No, he intended to enforce his will on *all* the classes, break their backs, crush their will to resist. As brutal as that sounded, he was convinced that only by instilling a climate conducive to learning would he actually be fulfilling his duty to these young men. Being cruel in order to be kind – yeah, in a way, yes. If this was breaking eggs to make an omelette, then that would vividly illustrate exactly what his intentions were. He managed to ease through the first day of classes with little open resistance, but, when reading the eyes of certain inmates, he knew that the coming weeks would test him again and again, with those inmates curious to see if he had the fortitude to tough out this test of wills.

Of course, there were other more mundane problems to bother him. In late March a storm past through the panhandle causing a small tornado to hit some land along highway 98 east of Marianna. Just to boot, Jim's back yard resembled a swimming pool after one particular heavy rain storm since the yard was slightly slanted down-hill, resulting in the water forming a huge pool along the neighbor's fence, not draining off for days. Even worse than that was discovery he made while clearing some small branches and leafs one Saturday afternoon. There he was, raking the back yard dressed in shorts and a T-shirt, minding his own business, lost in his thoughts, when he felt a sudden, sharp pain in his low right leg. Glancing down he saw a blur of yellow before being stung again...and again! Dropping his rake he fled around the house and hopped in his Karman Ghia, trying to figure out what had happened. Obviously some kind of wasps or hornets had attacked him, stinging him several times… and man did it hurt! He couldn't remember being stung like this since he was a small kid. Both legs too. After some thirty minutes the pain started to ease and he slipped out of the car and into the house. Later that evening his brother told him that the critters which had bitten him were ground wasps, who were known to be very aggressive when disturbed. Before going to bed Dick went out in the back yard armed with a flashlight, lighter fluid and matches. Quickly he found the small hole beside the rake, pumping gobs of the fluid into the hole. When lit, it cast a pale blue flame in the dark. They no longer had any problems with the ground wasps.

It didn't take long before the more inveterate inmates began testing him, bating him, pushing the envelop, to see how he would react. Using an old, standard-trick to goad him, a guy in one of the rear rows of the classroom would begin to whistle in a low, steady tone, ceasing, however, whenever Dick left his desk, attempting to detect the exact source of the sound. Suspecting, rightly so, that this was meant as an indirect challenge to his authority, Dick began to analyze the students one by one, sorting out those who were more or less friendly to him and those seemingly neutral. After a while he had narrowed the possible suspects down to four persons. The next day he ordered two of them to change seats, bringing them up to the front row, offering as an excuse, that he wanted to more closely observe their academic progress. Hardly had five minutes passed than the whistling began anew. Dick waited some seconds then, unexpectedly, called one of the suspected inmates up to the desk, ostensibly to have him take a "special test", devised to have him sit over in the other corner at a lone desk. Now all was still in the room. Three minutes later the "phantom whistler" once again announced his presence. His head bent down toward a book, Dick did his best to look upward unobtrusively, trying his damnest to finally pin down the exact location of the perpetrator. Then, over in the back row, on the left side – he could just make out the pursed lips of the inmate. That sufficed, and Dick's reaction was immediate. "Jackson! Get your ass up here now!" As the inmate slowly shuffled up to the front of the class, the others exchanged curious glances. What was going to happen now? How was this recalcitrant inmate going to be punished? It had taken a while for Dick to come up with an adequate form of punishment for minor misdemeanors like this one, but he had finally found what he thought (and what proved to be) a fair penalty for such an offense. As the malefactor stood unrepentant in front of him, Dick reamed him out: "O.K., you goddamned son of a bitch! You fucking wise-ass! Get your ass out the door and out on the plaza. Just sit on the goddamn bench! Just sit there and don't say a fucking word to *anybody* ... until I tell you to return to class. Got it?!" Dutifully Jackson went outside and sat down on the concrete bench. Dick let him roast for some thirty minutes before allowing Jackson back into class.

Although this may not have seemed like a harsh form of punishment, it actually was. The reason for this was two-fold. First off, the weather appeared to be hostile toward the inmates, either a scorching sun in the summer or cold and windy in the winter. Moreover, sitting desolately there on the bench, with no one to talk to, exposed as on a pillory - the inmate alone, frozen in time. This, plus a check mark by their name (which they had to initial), meant that they were just two more checks away from the front office. Being sent to the front office sounded more like school days, where one would receive a reprimand or maybe a letter for the parents regarding the student's misconduct. But no, here at ACI things were not so lenient, for being sent to the front office was tantamount to being *locked up!* For in those cases, inmates were placed behind bars, with the number of days being decided by the superintendent himself.

However, should he ever have entertained the thought of victory that first morning, he soon discovered, much to his chagrin, that he had indeed won a battle, but not the war, since many of the other classes had gone over to leading a type of guerrilla warfare of sorts, lurking, waiting for the slightest opportunity to outsmart their teacher. Sure enough, Friday morning in the first level class, which, because of its low academic achievement had two hours of class time broken by a fifteen minute break. Dick had just finished correcting a test, calling an inmate up to his desk to review the results, when the bell rang ending the second period. In a jiffy, a blue wave surged past the desk and out the door, leaving him alone. Pleased as punch to have some time to restore a semblance of order on desk, he suddenly realized that the answer sheet was missing! The same one used to correct the chapter test minutes ago. Desperately he scrounged around trying to locate it, all to no avail, until the blatant truth became too obvious to overlook. Joiner, the inmate he had just finished helping when the bell rang, must have used the commotion to swipe the sheet! Eyes ablaze with righteous anger he lunged out the door and onto the plaza, startling those inmates close by through his unexpected appearance. "Joiner, goddamn it, get your ass inside - now!", he roared, starting a small hubbub among the inmates, all now curious as to what would follow. Once inside again, Dick took the shaken young man into the long, narrow, windowless, side-room, far from any probing gazes from the plaza. He then proceeded to ream Joiner a new asshole, crucifying him verbally, cursing him for having the audacity (now he may have used the term balls) to attempt to *steal* the answer sheet off of the teacher's desk, Well, he'd better spread the gospel that a new show was in town now, move over rover was the motto, so if he wished to keep his young ass from *lock up* he'd better get on the stick quick! Joiner was told to initial the check by his name and sit out on the bench until called back into class. The whole event seemed to have a mollifying effect on the class, which was docile for weeks afterward.

Still tense from the hard day at work Dick looked forward to his running, which he had started back in the spring of 1967 and kept up in the following years in Florida, West Berlin and on Taiwan. Slipping into his shorts and T-shorts he took off down Decatur, turning right at Madison, taking a left at Kelsen Avenue, then onto state road 167 where he sprinted up the small hill on the left hand side. Really panting, sweating by now, he started the return trip home, having had lots of time to ruminate about his present situation, his future and even the world in general. Then, completely out of the blue, he began remembering an old song from his childhood days in Winter Haven, where the neighboring Bates family played their radio from morning to night. On one of those interminably sultry summer afternoons he recalled

having heard the following song by Webb Pierce wafting over the backyard and into the bedroom:

Well I once had a friend named Ramblin' Bob,
Who used to steal, gamble and rob,
He thought he was the smartest guy around,
But I found out last Monday, that Bob got locked up Sunday, They got him
in the jailhouse way downtown.

Chorus

He's in the jailhouse now,
He's in the jailhouse now,
I told him once or twice,
To quit playin' cards and shootin' dice, He's in the jailhouse now.

The song made him wince because he still found it hard to believe that
here, in the year 1975, he, of all people, should have ended up teaching
in a prison, since there was absolutely nothing in his cv pointing towards this ignominious fate. No, just the opposite! Why then did this
misfortune befall him, him who had planned for graduate school over
at FSU, a teaching assistantship in a Ph.D. program. Moan and groan as
he may, the decision by the Veteran's Administration to veto his plans
for using his remaining GI Bill money for grad school had torpedoed
his hopes for the time being, and he'd just have to deal with it, making
further plans right now on an ad hoc basis.

After a bracing shower he wandered into the kitchen to get a glass of
lime juice. Upon opening the refrigerator he noticed that there was *no*
beer. Not a big beer drinker himself, why should this be of any great
importance to him? Well, it seems as if his brother Jim and Phil
Corsmeier had had an argument about one of them having *no beer* on

the premise. As a result both agreed that they would *always* have beer in the fridge whenever the other happened to show up. Should one of them forget this, not having any beer in stock, then the poor fool would have to go out and buy a six- pack for both of them to share. Usually Jim was pretty sharp about keeping at least, a couple of cans cool, should his friend, "Philo", suddenly pull a surprise *raid* in Decatur Street. Wanting to warn is brother, Dick scribbled a note, saying that he'd better buy some beer pronto since, just like trailer parks attract tornados, a beerless fridge would definitely attract "Philo".

Easter came very early that year, so, with the temperatures rising, Jim was out canoeing with a friend on the Chipola on that Sunday, leaving Dick to his own devices, which meant working on his Chinese, puttering around the house, trying to find a decent program worth watching on TV (he soon gave up) or reading the latest edition of *Die Zeit*, him trying his best to keep up with events in Germany. Around 3:00 pm the phone rang, Dick being surprised to hear his Mom on the other end, telling her son to please sit down, she had some awful news for him. With no idea of what was to follow, he sat down on the living room couch, curious as to what this ominous news could be. As her voice choked up, the words stumbled out of the receiver in a blind rush. Radio; she had heard on the radio of a terrible shoot out in Louisiana, persons wounded, killed, by a sniper, a young man who later killed himself; a brief instant of silence, before she added, "It sounded like his name was Bob Howard." Dick froze, his grip on the phone tightened, not wanting to believe what he had just heard, merely able to croak out a desperate, "Are you *sure*?" His Mom stammered something about how he should listen to the latest radio news reports for further information and, not wanting to heighten the emotional stress on her son, she hung up, saying that he should keep in touch.

That afternoon seemed to stretch out endlessly, with no one to talk to, no person to commiserate with him, leaving him alone with his memories. He and Bob had been high school friends, with Bob being a top student, an avid chess player and an assistant to the chemistry teacher. Two years later, after Dick had finished his active duty with the Navy, they had roomed together for two and a half years off-campus in Gainesville. Arriving back at the university for the Fall trimester 1965, Dick was shocked to hear that Bob had failed to register for classes, telling Dick he'd like to take a break from his studies, you know, work a little at Shelley's (a pub close to campus), smoke a little dope and take it easy. Now sporting long hair and wearing sandals, Bob fulfilled the description of what one was beginning to call the *hippies*. Bob was scared to death that the draft board would soon contact him regarding a possible coming induction into the US Army, meaning, with the increasing escalation of the war in Vietnam, an increasing threat that he'd be sent overseas and into combat. Appalled at this thought, Bob left Gainesville in the spring of 1966, heading for New York, planning to *disappear* for awhile. When Dick and his buddy Al visited New York in the spring of 1967 they found Bob living in a tiny apartment, heavily involved in the local drug scene and already beginning to show signs of growing paranoia. Before leaving the states for Berlin in late March of 1968, Dick had flown to New York where he spent a short week at Bob's pad, a larger apartment, housing a handful of fellow drug users. By this time Bob was so strung out that when the draft board finally caught up with him and demanded that he take a physical, he readily agreed, proudly producing two arms chock-full of track marks from injections. That, plus a short interview with a psychiatrist, was enough to have him classified 4F, with him no longer considered fit for use by the army; however, his life was now a complete mess. Imagine Dick's surprise (and chagrin) when Bob suddenly popped up in West Berlin in June 1970. By now Bob was popping Valium, drinking lots of beer while attempting to keep his paranoid mind under control. After jaunts to various countries such as Sweden, Denmark and Holland, where he would immediately seek out the local drug scene, he returned to West Berlin a wreck, with him in the late fall soon being placed in a psychiatric clinic not far from the student village where Dick lived. Neither that clinic nor the psychiatrists at the US Army hospital could provide the care needed, thus the US consulate turned out to be kind enough to offer him a small loan so Bob could purchase a flight back to the states. Years later, in the fall of 1974 Dick received a short letter from Bob describing his new life in Colorado. No more hard drugs, just pot and Valium. He was living with a bunch of hippies in a sort of camp and had just broken up with his girl friend. He mentioned having visited his mom down in Monroe, Louisiana.

Bit by bit the whole ugly story was revealed by the press. Evidently Bob had returned home in mid-March to Monroe, where his mom and her new husband were living. Then, without warning, early Easter afternoon he had somehow gotten his hands on one of his step father's rifles and shells, going up to attic, where from the window, he had an unobstructed view of the street below. opening fire on the unsuspecting pedestrians, killing two innocent persons and seriously wounding a third, after which he turned the gun on himself, committing suicide. Normally this event would have made nation headlines; however, this was not to be since on the very same afternoon as Bob was shooting at passersby in Monroe, another man in Ohio was going on a murderous rampage shooting eleven members of his family in a huge bloodbath.

When Jim finally got home that evening he winced on hearing the bad news, having known Bob fairly well and saw in him, as so many friends and teachers, a young man bound for success in the field of chemistry. Over a cold beer Dick reiterated all facts known at present, trying his best to bear the loss of a close friend with a modicum of self-control, attempting to once again regain the poise he had lost that afternoon.

Perhaps unwittingly Jim came to his aid in remarking that he well remembered Bob water skiing out at the Park's house on Lake Cannon Drive, telling Dick that that was the way he'd aways remember Bob, cruising on to the beach on his slalom spraying a bright sheet of water to brake his speed just before reaching the shore. Tanned, sporty and smart, that was the picture Jim said would remain in his memory. Seeing the inherent wisdom contained in the statement, Dick felt constrained to agree. Yeah, that was the answer, accentuate the positive; still, the grief and pain remained, even if gradually dimming, since the world didn't stop spinning and other events soon attracted his attention.

By now the morning drive over to ACI more or less resembled a funeral because the 6:30 news was reporting on a constantly deteriorating situation in Vietnam, with the south Vietnamese army now reeling under a full-blown, all out offensive by the north. Slouched in the their seats, the passengers were bombarded daily with depressing reports – DaNang overrun by enemy troops, shortly afterwards followed the stunning loss of Cam Ranh Bay, once a major US base. Much as boxers hanging on the ropes taking shot after shot, they listened quietly, stolid faced, to the *Götterdämmerung* taking place thousands of miles away in southeast Asia, witnessing the final act of the Vietnam drama. Dick found a vicarious pleasure in watching the fellow riders twitch with every body-shot, didn't they have it coming? All of these super- patriotic, jingoist, conservative southerners were blind to US imperialism abroad, just as they were supporting the everyday racism in their own country. Well, as a certain Malcom X once said: "Now the chickens are coming home to roost."

Krakatoa Reloaded

In the weeks following Easter the internecine struggle in the the classroom continued, with the combat taking many turns, both sides convinced that they were on the long end of the stick, thinking the other side would quit and call it a day. Nevertheless, Dick sensed a victory slowly coming into view because, of the ten classes, there were five or six who were now toeing the line, more or less requiring less energy in reprimanding them, thus leaving him free to concentrate on the other, more refractory ones. One class in particular proved to be a hard nut to crack. The main instigator was a burly young black inmate with the name of Delozer, who delighted in making Dick's life miserable. By mid-April Dick had succeeded in breaking the will of all the classes, now having them march to his drumbeat, follow his lead – that is all except one, and that was a low level class held in the afternoon. While drawing a diagram up on the greenboard, with his back turned to the inmates an object went hurtling by his head splattering against the greenboard. Spinning around to spot the culprit, he was greet by hoots of derision, a phalanx of malicious faces, no one about to give the slightest hint of who the perpetrator was. Still, Dick had figured out roughly from the splotch that the trajectory of the object must have come from the right side of the classroom. Secondly, he knew his inmates, thus he could narrow down the number of suspicious persons to two or three, one of them being, of course, Delozer. After class was over, the cleaning team came in, a group of three inmates who would sweep and swab down the room during the hour break. One of them quickly sussed out the origin of the object thrown – a small chicken egg. Thankful for the tip, Dick then walked over to the admin building to find out which inmates were working over at the chicken farm. And guess what? On the short list of workers stood the name Delozer. So, so thought Dick, already trying to set up in his mind a plan for the next day.

In many ways ACI was just an innocent victim of the economic recession hitting the US, supposedly the worse since the end of WW II. In addition to this, Nixon's war on drugs program saw the incarceration of thousands of persons nationwide for relatively small, petty misdemeanors. One of the inmates from the Florida panhandle had told Dick that he'd been arrested for possessing *two* marijuana cigarettes! That alone meant *three* years at ACI! Many of the inmates hailed from the larger centers of population, Dade, Broward, Hillsborough or Duval county, which also meant, implicitly, that they were *black*. There was also a sprinkling of hispanic inmates, perhaps 5%. The recession had put a crunch on the job market, further reducing the already few chances for blacks to gain employment. Again and again Dick would hear the same story from black inmates from the metropolitan areas; if you wanted to earn money in the ghettos, particularly quick money, well, the only real options open were armed robbery, drugs, prostitution or gambling. Some of the hispanics had told him they had been involved in *bolita*, a numbers game. Any way you sliced it, it all made common sense to those hanging around in the streets, with little skills and education. One didn't need a Ph.D. to grasp the essence of the problem.

During the morning classes Dick mulled over the problem of actually catching Delozer in flagranti, red-handed, in the act; in fact, the more he considered it, the more difficult it became to work out a solution promising a successful outcome. All through the lunch break he tried to no avail to figure out a strategy; so when the class started, he really had no clear idea of what he'd do during the next hour. Then, a half an hour later, out of desperation, an idea came to him. What he'd do was this – he would basically repeat his actions of the other day, drawing a diagram on the chalkboard with his back turned toward the inmates.

Occasionally and without warning he would turn around to explain some detail to his listeners. In doing this he could also surmise as to whether Delozer might be preparing his "egg attack". Thus Dick commenced to tell the class that some inmates had told him they hadn't grasped all the details of yesterday's explanation, with him now ready to repeat the performance. No sooner had he begun, he suddenly pivoted around, to explain some minor point, indirectly scanning the rear seats where Delozer was sitting. It seemed to Dick as if the young man was looking froggy, so he turned back to the chalk board, drawing, but also slowly counting up to ten, then pivoting around again just in time to see the egg fly by some six inches from his nose, again splattering against the board. However, he had turned just in time to see Delozer trying to slip unnoticed back on his seat. Confidently, without the slightest trace of anger, he walked over to his desk and sat down. The room was silent. Without raising his voice he looked over at the perpetrator, stating calmly that he wished to see him after class. The last thirty minutes transpired uneventfully. After the bell had rung and the inmates had left the room, Delozer strolled up to the desk with the innocent face of a cherub, when the following conversation ensued:

Delozer (a bit sullenly): "Whut you callin' me up here fo'?"

Dick: "You damned well know why I called your ass up here."

Delozer (petulantly): "Watfo', ah didn't do nuthin'?"

Dick (now peeved): "You fucking smart ass. You threw those chicken eggs. I *saw* you trying to slip back to your seat! Now why the hell did you do a stupid thing like that?"

Delozer (sullen again): "Ain't none of yo' business."

Dick: "Goddamn it, I'm making it my business, you stupid son-of-a-bitch! Now tell me something you miserable shit-head – do you want to go into *lock up*? Huh, now do ya?"

At that very moment Dick perceived it, the slight quiver or twitch which crossed the young man's face, announcing silently that his threat had scored a bullseye, a direct hit. Toning language down a bit, Dick now proceeded to offer a glimmer of hope.

Dick: "Well, I'll tell ya what I'm gonna do. I'm gonna give you *one* more chance to keep your young ass out of the slammer. Now you're gonna sit tight from now on, right? Work through your chapters so you can pass your GED test, right? I can't hear your answer, speak up god-dammit!"

Delozer (nodding): "Yeah, yeah. I got the message."

Dick: "That's not what I want to know, dammit. What I wanta know is, are you gonna really *do* this - or are you only tryin' to bullshit me?"

Delozer (quietly): "No, no I'm not bullshit'in."

Putting two big checks by his name, Dick made extra sure that the inmate saw that he was now at the edge of an abyss.

Dick: "Now initial this. Is it clear that the next fuck up means *lock up?*"

Delozer: "Yassir."

Dick: "O.K. From now on I expect some *extra effort* from you because we have a lot of work to catch up on, right?"

Delozer: "I suppose you're right."

Dick: "Don't *suppose!* I am right goddammit! Now get out of here, I got work to do."

That same evening he told Jim that he thought he had reached a turning point, that within the next week he'd finally be able to really spend his time teaching instead of wasting his time imposing discipline on the classes. His brother mentioned that he was glad to hear this since he knew that Dick had been under a lot of pressure in the past months and was pleased to hear of this positive turn of events. Sleep came easily too that night, with Dick blissfully thinking that the worst was over, that his hopes for the future weren't just merely a chimera or will-o'-the-wisp, but were real; thus just before dozing off to sleep, he started concocting concrete plans for the near future.

At the end of April two events from abroad made major stories in the newspapers as well as on radio and TV. The *RAF* (*Red Army Faction*) stormed the West German embassy in Stockholm demanding the release of several *RAF* members in prison, including Baader and Meinhof. After a diplomat was shot to death, Chancellor Helmut Schmidt rejected any plans to negotiate with the *RAF*, a diplomat was executed in front of an open window, causing the Swedish police to plan an attack, but before they could, two massive explosions were set off by the terrorists later executing another West German diplomat. Two terrorists were also killed during the attack. Amazed at the effrontery of the RAF in attacking the West German embassy in politically neutral Sweden, Dick cursed the whole pack of bourgeois *Kinder* wanting to play *Tupomeros* in Scandinavia, murdering innocent people, blowing up a whole damned embassy. This was exactly the type of action which alienated the public, allowing the police to arm themselves even further, permitting politicians to suggest restricting civil rights by introducing laws to increasing government surveillance of private communication. Well, he couldn't spend too much time worrying over this matter, seeing as he himself had his hands full with his inmates, particularly in the past weeks when an early Florida summer was on them revving up the temperatures, of both the heavy, moist air, plus the tension in the overcrowded prison.

Riding to work that last week in April meant that each morning the riders were subjected to a constant avalanche of news reports from Vietnam, where an endgame scenario was quickly unfolding with the complete collapse of the south Vietnamese army, north Vietnamese tanks punching holes through the thin lines surrounding Saigon, finally grinding into the capital itself. Terrible scenes had taken place, South Vietnamese clinging desperately to the skids of US helicopters lifting the last refugees from the roof the the US embassy, deadly afraid of being captured by the Communists. So, some ten years after the big escalation and Johnson's "we will stand in Vietnam", everything had disintegrated into chaos, with literally every man for himself. Bitterly Dick regarded this disaster as further proof that the war was truly unwinnable right from the start, not wanting to admit his early support for the war in the first stages, in fact, not ready to admit that the game wasn't worth the candle until the fall of 1967, when taking an anti-war stance had gained a wide following, No, he had never been actively involved in the civil rights movement nor with the dissidents of the Vietnam war. Nevertheless, he enjoyed the vicarious pleasure of watching the men around him winch and twitch as the full panorama of utter defeat was fed to them on a daily basis, much like a child having to swallow a bitter medicine it doesn't like. During the news the car was silent, as if an appalling dirge were being played. Dick had never experienced anything like this in his entire life. The sultry morning had passed by uneventfully and, after lunch, the short break found Dick in the library leafing through some magazines, enjoying the cool, dry air, the peace and quietness of the room. Then suddenly, the door opened, one of the men from administration, gray haired, with wire-frame glasses, who Dick vaguely knew, stuck his head in the door, looking rapidly around the room. "Any women in here?" he queried. Then he was gone, leaving Dick to wonder what this was all about since he'd never seen the man outside of the admin building before; moreover, what was the meaning of that strange question "are there any women in here?" Gradually he felt a growing uneasiness, hard to pin down exactly, but becoming ever stronger. Tossing the magazine aside, he shoved the heavy metal door open, turning to his right, now at the corner of the building, where he ran into a sheer wall of sound! He felt the hairs on his neck stand on end by the sheer intensity of this disharmonious caterwaul, at times resembling a wail, only to shift into a howl, a sound he had *never* heard before. Turning the corner he glimpsed the cause: a flood of inmates sprinting across grass heading for the construction site, with Dick unable to fathom the reason for this act. What had happened? What was the root cause? From the admin building he saw a lonely, solitary figure step outside, a security guard, with a helmet, protective vest and a rifle. Dick asked himself how in God's name could this one individual ever hope to quell the unrest which had broken out? Just then another man from the administration ran by him, telling him to return to his classroom and lock the door behind him; good advice, which Dick promptly followed. Of course, classes were cancelled for the rest of the day with the classroom teachers still in the dark about what had caused the disturbance and what counter-measures had been taken. That evening, over a cold beer, he reiterated to his brother the startling events of the day, Jim completely agog at the news, wanting to know more details from Dick, who, unfortunately, was unable to provide them, merely adding that he would definitely find out the next day. Upon his arrival early the next morning he found the following newsletter lying on his desk:

May 5, 1975

TO:	**INMATE POPULATION**
FROM:	**SUPERINTENDENT**
SUBJECT:	**Tension Among Inmate Population**

During the past few days it is apparent that there has been mounting tension among the inmate population. The staff is of the opinion that such tension is manifested in the attempts of a few inmates to disrupt the normal operation by pulling into their ranks as many other inmates as possible in order to create a problem. I feel that it is my responsibility, not as a threat, but to advise each of you of Florida Statue 944.45, reference mutiny, riot, strike; and penalty –

> "Whoever instigates, contrives, willfully attempts to cause, assists, or conspires to cause any mutiny, riot, or strike in defiance of official orders in any state correctional institution, shall be guilty of a felony of the second degree, punishable as provided in 775.082". (A felony of the second degree is punishable by a tern [sic] of imprisonment in the state prison not to exceed fifteen (15) years.)

I strongly urge each of you to consider the many factors in your individual case, to act on your own behalf, and not be misled by a few who wish to use you for support. If you are capable of making your own choices in life, then let no one use you to support their choices. I offer this advise in sincere hope that you will use your own mind to make those choices that will be beneficial and in your best interest.

HAVE A BEST DAY

Garrie Curlee, Superintendent

GC: elm

During each class the next morning he began questioning the more trustworthy inmates as to the reason behind yesterday's disturbance, which he later surmised had actually evolved into a full-scale riot. After talking to five or six inmates, black and white, the scattered facts slowly congealed into the following picture. One of the new inmates, a young, naive white kid, had gotten up out of bed around 3:00 am in the morning to go to the toilette. Once there, he was accosted by three or four black inmates who proceeded to rape him. Early that same morning, the young inmate had managed to craft himself a "shank", prison parlance for a type of of self-made knife constructed out of razor blades, wood and tape. Around noon he spotted the person, or one of the persons, who he thought had raped him, attacking him without warning, stabbing him in the chest. This act immediately incited a fight, which quickly spread, pitting black against white. Unfortunately, during this melee, the inmates had neglected the young man who had been stabbed and who lay there bleeding profusely. By the time inmates had notified the infirmary and a doctor had managed to arrived on the scene, the poor inmate was dead. That was the primary cause of the riot which broke out a short time later. Dick was told that the scene he had witnessed yesterday had been the flight of the white inmates heading for the construction site in order to arm themselves. Luckily for all involved, the security guards were able to quell the riot before anyone was killed, although some of the white inmates were severely beaten up by enraged blacks. It wasn't until his 11:00 am class arrived in the classroom that he was told the terrible news, namely that the inmate killed yesterday was no other than Steve Hollie, who had sat there in the same room, same seat just the other day. Steve appeared to be a fairly well adjusted person, not particularly aggressive, relatively reliable in finishing his class work punctually, seemingly not easily peeved or upset. During the next hour Dick was merely ephemerally aiding inmates, correcting their tests, whereas really his mind was gyrating wildly, trying in vain to come up with a credible answer as to whether Steve was really involved in the incident. Of course, his first thought was to reject any involvement whatsoever. How could this young, nice man have ever done such a repugnant deed? But then who was he to judge? Had he been there? Had he spoken with anyone witnessing the act? He knew from his old US Navy days aboard a ship how horny men could become; however, the longest extend period had been the "shakedown cruise" down to Guantanamo Bay for merely some six weeks, no longer. Here at ACI you had young men sentenced to prison terms up to three or four years, living in over-crowded conditions in over-heated quarters; consequently, sodomy in prisons was nothing new under the sun. Nevertheless, Dick actively sought some kind of a solution which could lift the blame on his student. Had Steve actively participated, or was a merely a passive observer? Did the act take place in semi-darkness? Was the victim sure that Steve was one of the assailants or was he really just out for revenge, thinking he had stabbed one of the *real* perpetrators? By the time the bell rang, ending the class, Dick found himself no closer to a solution, perhaps in fact, totally lost in a quandary, unsure of what to believe.

While eating lunch he felt some one tapping him on the shoulder, much to his surprise it turned out to be Mr. Sexton, the educational supervisor, who informed him that Dick was to meet him in the main office of the admin building immediately after finishing his lunch, an unexpected invitation which left Dick puzzled. Why this meeting and what about his afternoon classes? Others, now aware that something very unusual was coming off, offered their own theories as to the reason for this occurrence, all convinced that it had something to do with yesterday's events, but no one quite sure as to what this meeting would entail.

By 1:00 pm all those invited were assembled in Mr. Sexton's office, about fourteen persons in altogether, and all males. Among them were two teachers, Dick, Lawton and a man from the main office named Mel. Turning toward the three, Mr. Sexton reminded them sternly that, whether they remembered it or not, in signing their contracts they had also agreed to a provision dealing with prison security. In case of a major disturbance within ACI, teaching personnel could be compelled to participate in enforcing the security measures decided upon by the superintendent himself. Surveying the group with a steely glance, Mr. Sexton, asked if there were any questions concerning that which he had just said. In the silence that followed Dick noticed a stricken look among the teachers, who had never imagined that they would find themselves in such a prickly situation, with no other real alternative but to obey those orders rendered by the ACI direction. Mr. Sexton then led the group into a small armory, explaining that they were about to be armed in order to serve as a sort of auxiliary force, supplementing the regular staff and given a more or less passive role. That said, bulletproof vests were passed around, proof enough that the situation was indeed serious. Throats became dryer, hands clammier, as the shotguns came out of storage, with each person being handed a 12 gauger. In his youth Dick and his brothers had done some shooting with their grandfather's rifles, mostly only using the 22's, having fired the shotguns or the 30-30 just a couple of times, thus the feel of the gun in his hands didn't really give him the willies – as was visibly the case with the two other teachers. Before loading the rifles, all were told to keep the safety on, not to release them unless one intended to shoot. The crowning moment arrived when the ammunition was passed around and the guns loaded. Dutifully following one of the security guards, the three men marched off towards the classrooms, cutting straight across the broad plaza to the far corner, where two steel doors led out onto a field used for exercising, running and other sports. There they stopped, with the guard giving them final instructions. It seemed as if some inmates had planned on rioting sometime that very afternoon. At present it was unclear as to just how many might follow them, perhaps with some kind of self-made weapons. Now this was where the teachers came into the plan. Handbills had been printed and decimated among the inmates making it clear that those inmates *not* ready to participate in any type of illegal disturbance should walk over to the education area where they would be safe from any marauding inmates set on violence. Wishing the three young men lots of luck, the guard marched off leaving the trio alone on a hot, steamy afternoon.

Silently the men gazed at one another, then turning quickly away, seeing that their counterparts were just as nervous as they were. All knew that it was just a matter of time, maybe fifteen minutes, perhaps a half an hour before all hell would break loose.

They were paralyzed by the thought of half-crazed inmates bursting through the unlocked doors in one gigantic wave! What were they to do? How best to handle this ungodly situation which none of them had ever imagined, much less experienced? In this growing tension Dick, seeing that he was the oldest (if only slightly) among the three, broke the deadening silence:

Dick (dourly): "Well, we'd better start planning what we're gonna do when the riot jumps off."

Lawton (warily): "What ya mean? You gotta plan?"

Dick: "Lemme tell you something, man. When those inmates come runnin' through those doors there's gonna be hell to pay if we don't figure out some kinda plan of action now, and quick!"

Meanwhile Mel is just looking down forlornly at his shoelaces, obviously not wanting the others to work matters out.

Lawton: "O.K., you got any wise ideas 'bout what to do?"

Now the ball had landed on Dick's court, forcing him to rapidly find some kind of equitable solution that would provide safety for the inmates and also security for the three teachers.

Dick (decidedly): "My plan is this: Mel, you go over there to the right... about five yards from the door. I'll stand here on the left side. Lawton, you go back out on the plaza, where there's lots of room. Now, when the inmates start coming through the doors, Mel and I will order them to go out on the plaza, to sit down and not move! Lawton, it'll be your job to keep 'em under control. Y'all got it?"

Lawton (whining): "Why *me*?"

Dick (angrily): "O.K. Goddammit, then you switch places with Mel. Then *you'll* have to face those inmates when they coming pouring through the doors!"

Lawton (reconsidering): "Well, well maybe you're right. Yeah, I'll stand back and guard 'em while you and Mel steer 'em over out on the plaza."

Mel, with a stricken look plastered over his young face, now begins to peep up in a quavering voice.

Mel: "I, I definitely agree with both of you. But, one thing really bothers me."

Dick: "Yeah. What?"

Mel (hesitantly): "Well, you know when the inmates come through the doors … and we tell them to go out onto the plaza and sit down, right? I mean, well, that's what we tell them, right?"

Dick (peeved): "So, what's the problem?"

Mel suddenly seemed to be overwhelmed by the heebie-jeebies, his eyes rolling around, his voice starting to crack.

Mel: "Well, w-what happens if they don't obey - I, I mean what if they just *keep coming* at me. Well, what should I *do*?"

Complete silence. Yeah, what *should* they do in the worst case scenario. When push came to shove. This was the crux of the matter, this was why they had been armed.

Dick (slowly): "Well, one thing's for damned sure. I'm not gonna let an inmate take my rifle away from me … hell, he could shoot me with it! I'm gonna do this: when they come through the doors I keep the rifle up high and tell 'em what to do. If they don't follow my commands, I'll lower the rifle towards them, warning that if they come any closer I'll shoot!"

Lawton: "I agree. If they don't stop, well, *they have it coming.*"

Mel (plaintively): "Yeah, then, then they've *asked for it.*"

The miasmal shroud of fear and doubt, the visceral reaction to an imminent, likely violent confrontation, gradually subsided in the tranquillity of a torpid Florida summer afternoon, it now being replaced by a certain displeasure in having to wait in vain for something to occur, some event which would call for action, yes, some form of excitement;

almost anything was better than just standing idly around, pockets of sweat starting to form bloches under their armpits, the shotguns feeling heavier with every minute. Languidly at first, then slowly morphing into a sharper tone, the exasperated trio began to verbally rev things up, anything to break increasing dissatisfaction with the dullness of their task. In doing this, they now began shifting the blame onto the inmates.

Lawton (grumpy): "Damn, we've been out here for at least an hour, just swatting flies. If those guys wanna riot, well, let 'em start. I'm tired of just standing around with my finger up my ass. Hell, I say, Let it happ'n Capt'n!"

Dick (pointing his gun at the door): "Well, the first guy who comes through the door is gonna seen *my* gun aimed at his guts, with me tellin' him to get his young ass out on the plaza! Mel, you ready too?"

Mel (grimly): "Yep, I'm ready."

Dick: "And what about you, Lawton? You up to snuff?"

Lawton (adamantly): "You're goddamn right I am! I'm tired of this dip-shit game the inmates are playin'. Fuck 'em! Let 'em come, the sooner the better!"

Mel: "I say let's get this over with. Get the show on the road!"

Lawton (calling over to Dick): "Why don't you open one of those doors 'n take a quick peek outside?"

Slowly opening one of the doors Dick made a swift check of the area.

Dick (shaking his head): "Nope, narry a person in sight."

An extended period of silence.

Mel (tentatively): "And what is if they *don't* come?"

A long pause ensues. Until now no one has broached this question.

Dick: "Well, we can't *force* them to come in, right?"

Lawton: "Well, then what in hell are we doin' out here? Waitin' for the sun to go down? I'm tired of this rinky-dink shit. What in the hell did they *arm* us for? Let's get this goddamn thing over so we can head home!"

Mel (chiming in): "You're right. I don't see much sense in what we're doing?"

Dick (reluctantly): "We can't leave until we've been relieved."

Lawton: "Lord 'a mercy, what a way to spend a damn afternoon."

Around 5:30 pm one of the correction officers appeared, telling them to turn in their vests and shotguns at the admin building and that they were now free to return home. Not sure as to whether they were to regard themselves as heroes or stooges, the trio split up, each one tired and hungry, still mulling over what they had just experienced.

Having been informed the prior evening about the tense situation at ACI, Jim didn't seem surprised at all to see his brother come through the front door some two hours later than usual. He did, however, express a keen interest in Dick's long-winded story about standing guard, armed with loaded shotguns. Yep, that surely grabbed his attention. Later, Dick counter-balanced this tale, telling his brother that he had gained some valuable insight that afternoon, unfortunately, the new perspective being rather pessimistic. When Jim asked just what that could be, his brother replied that, for the first time, he could understand the problem of soldiers, who, for lack of war, just hung around the barracks, facing months of tedious boredom, looking forward to some action, to be finally *doing what they had been trained for*! Young men froggy for real action! Almost embarrassed now, he described to Jim the initial gnawing fear which had gradually given way to a suffocating sense of monotony; which, in turn, was transformed into a state of masculine cockiness, where the three armed teachers had begun bantering around, stating their readiness to *kick ass and take names* when the riot should jump off. Why, *hell yes*, weren't the inmates practically *asking for it! They* were the ones at fault! Jim, listening stone-faced, asked Dick if push had come to shove, would he have pulled the trigger, actually shoot an unarmed inmate. His brother's hesitant answer was that he was awful glad he didn't have to make that decision. Nevertheless, perhaps, had it come to a real melee that afternoon, well, he might have indeed pulled the trigger. In the silence that followed, Jim nodded his head slightly with Dick unable to discern whether his brother was expressing agreement or total disbelief.

In class the next day, Dick noted to his dismay that one of his favorite students, a young fellow by the name of Kip was missing – an ominous sign. When he later asked one of the other inmates for an explanation he was told that Kip had been right in the midst of the riot and was presently in the infirmary slowly recovering from the severe beating he had taken the day before yesterday, having found himself surrounded by a host of hostile black inmates, all eager to take their anger out on him. Kip of all people; Dick had likened him jokingly to one of the Munchkins from the old Wizard of Oz film since black-haired, blue-eyed Kip stood at a mere five feet four at best, with a friendly demeanor. Feeling some kind of vague responsibility for one of his better students, Dick decided to visit him during the lunch break.

Even beforehand it had been difficult for a teacher to move around freely outside of the education compound with the exceptions of the cafeteria or admin building, thus he was pleased when given permission to visit the infirmary right away, particularly when Dick said he was visiting one of his inmate-students, a riot victim at that. Easing into the room where Kip was laying, he was greeted warmly by a crooked smile and bright blue eyes. Only twice in his life had he ever seen a person as badly beaten. Once standing watch on the stern of the aircraft carrier anchored in Guantanamo Bay, he had seen a sailor being taken back to the ship from shore, in such terrible shape that he had to be hoisted aboard by placing two stokes' stretchers together, literally encasing the young man in a coffin-like web of wire-mesh; the other incident had taken place in West Berlin some three years ago, when an ex-convict from East Germany had turned upon a buddy, beating him so severely that the man's head ended up resembling a swollen, malformed football. Luckily Kip's face, while definitely showing signs of the beating he'd received, was still recognizable, even if he had to make a pronounced effort to speak distinctly through his swollen lips. After a short, five minute conversation, Dick was astonished to hear that his student held no grudges against those inmates that had attacked and savaged him. Kip summed things up rather succinctly in stating that he had simply *been at the wrong place at the wrong time*. Moved by this unexpected magnanimous interpretation of events, Dick promised to work closely with him in the future so that Kip could past the GED test. Walking back to his classroom, Dick ruminated over the short conversation, not able to imagine that he himself could have mustered up an equivalent generosity in such a case. In theory perhaps, but not in practice.

Foxtrot Corpen

Contrary to all his expectations (and fears), the riot appeared to have calmed things down for the time being, with some of the inmates coming to the conclusion that it could have been them who were victims of a "shank" attack. Moreover, the flyer issued by the Superintendent Curlee made it absolutely clear that those inmates guilty of instigating a mutiny, riot or strike would be charged with committing a second degree felony, a crime facing a prison term of up to fifteen years. Now even some of the hot-heads appeared to cool down. By the middle of May, Dick had all of his classes more or less under his (increasingly benevolent) control, with him finally having more time to concentrate on teaching. Toward the end of May he was surprised to be handed a copy of his Employee Service Rating as a Classroom Teacher II, particularly so when he read the remark "very knowledgeable in the subject matter he teaches". That was a real wowser! Just how in hell did they know of his teaching abilities? Were they questioning inmates? He seriously doubted that. How then could they know? Two days later during lunch he sought out Mr. Sexton, asking him obliquely how they knew that he was doing a good job teaching class. Smiling mysteriously, his boss told him not to worry, adding, "we have our own ways".

Merely some days after Dick found himself talking to Lawton about one of the latter's inmates, who was giving the teacher fits. Although Lawton had considered having the fellow locked up, he hesitated, mentioning that this might hinder him receiving a good service rating. On hearing this, Dick posed him the following question:

Dick: "Well, what I'd like to know is how exactly they calculate our ability as teachers? GED test results? Do they interview the inmates? What's the deal here?"

Lawton: "Very simple. Didn't you see the different categories on your sheet?"

Dick: "I already know that, but how do *they* know how I'm teaching?"

Lawton (in a burst of loud laughter): "Oh, my God. Mann, you've been eaten up with the dumb ass! Christ almighty, just what the hell do you think the loudspeaker in our rooms are for?!"

Loudspeakers? Oh so slowly it became painfully clear to him. Yeah, up above the greenboard, hardly ever used at all. In fact, so seldom that he had, in his constant conflicts with the inmates actually forgotten all about it.

Dick (hesitant): "...do you really think … ?"

Lawton: "Goddamn but you're stupid! Why they're always listening in, several times a day. Now don't tell me you never noticed this."

Dick: "Well, … "

Lawton (shaking his head): "I can't believe it! Mann you're so fucking naive!"

Dick (awkwardly): "O.K. I've learned my lesson. In the future I'll be more careful."

Lawton: "Listen to me. Don't ever forget rule number 1 at ACI – always keep your ass covered."

On the way back to Marianna that late afternoon he rummaged around in his mind, trying to review the past months. Lawton was right, Dick *did* remember times when, in the background, he had perceived a seemingly distant clicking noise, very faint. Not only once. However, he'd been too busy to worry about it, he had more pressing problems to deal with. Well, tomorrow he'd see Mr. Sexton at lunch, asking him directly for the truth of the matter. Dick was curious if the man would admit secretly spying on his teachers or perhaps attempt to somehow weasel his way out.

After lunch Dick intercepted Mr. Sexton as he was leaving the cafeteria, heading for his office in the admin building. Without further ado, Dick asked him point blank if some one was occasionally "listening in" on ongoing events in his classroom? Giving Dick a completely nonplussed look, he replied that "this was done often *as a matter of course.* This redounded naturally to the benefit of all the teachers, guaranteeing their *security!*" Speechless, Dick had to admit that the man had a point. Security was, of course, an overriding concern. With the wind having been taken out of his sails, Dick defeatedly slunk back to his classroom, feeling somewhat of a fool.

That evening at home saw Dick working on his Chinese, trying his best to extend his vocabulary, then, becoming tired of this, picking up a copy of *Die Zeit* to inform himself about the news from Germany. Around 9:00 pm Jim stormed into the house obviously in a state of anger. Stalking into the kitchen he whipped up a quick meal, bolting it down in large gulps. From his demeanor Dick could see that his brother was teed off, wisely deciding to wait until the emotional storm had calmed down some. Some ten minutes later he found himself sitting in the living room quietly listening to his brother's bitter reproach regarding the events which had just transpired that same evening. Jim had been dating a young woman for weeks, so as a sign of his growing interest he agreed to drive over to Chipley, where his girlfriend had a softball game. The girl, not at all bad looking, stood around five feet nine, was the team's pitcher. Although not so keen on ball sports, Jim had gladly opted to come out to this game, since he only considered it decent to support his new girlfriend and her team. Maybe the fact that her team lost the game had something to do with it; at any rate afterward she and Jim got into an argument about some actually mundane matter, but which ended up in a shouting match, where Jim felt that she had made some uncalled for, baseless critical remarks about him. On the drive back home Jim started to wind down, using the car ride to analyze the reasons for his girlfriend's outburst. As a result he came to the conclusion that the core-reason for the drama lay in the tense and tumulus relationship which the young lady had with her father. Because of this Jim had decided to terminate the relationship here and now, considering a further continuation really failed to make any sense. Tossing Dick a mournful glance he added that anytime Dick got serious about a woman, well, he should first off observe how she treated her own father. With tonight's story still ringing in his mind, Dick took this advice to heart, figuring it was straight out of the school of hard knocks, thus important to remember in similar future situations.

Through his multitude of friends and relations in Tallahassee Jim had heard through the grapevine that, Bob Eaglehart, one of Dick's old high school pals was now living out on highway 27 just north of Tally in a small town named Havana. Of course the local inhabitants, pulling a southern drall on the name, pronounced it *hey*-vana. Having also obtained Bob's telephone number, Jim passed it onto Dick, knowing that, particularly after Bob Howard's untimely demise, Dick would be glad to see an old friend from high school days… and beyond. The next weekend, following Bob's directions, Dick drove over to Havana to have a gander at the new house Bob and some friends had erected out in the boondocks. At first he thought he had been given false directions since the road was unpaved, red clay, full of ruts, partially washed out in places, causing the lower chassis of his baby-blue Karmann Ghia to almost run aground. "Goddamn", he thought, "some one should take care of this road, it being in such a pitiful condition." Upon reaching Bob's house he parked the car, stepping out to gaze at the unusual structure. And because he had built the house in a small gulch-like area, Bob had solved the problem posed by summer deluges in Florida by building the small wooden house on stilts, each of which were at least some twelve inches in diameter and over six feet tall. The interior was simple, but cozy. Dick felt at home right away, with Bob placing a cold beer in his hand, introducing him to friends from Tally who had come to visit him for the weekend.

Dick soon found himself involved in a conversation with one the guests, who was curious as to how one of Bob's friends should have ended up working, of all places, in a *prison*! In order to give him more context as to how he had happened on this particular job, Dick began more or less telling the guy his life story, emphasizing, of course, his Florida roots, especially stressing his years at the University of Florida in the mid-sixties. Wanting to add a dash of empathy, he also mentioned that all of his brothers (the traitors!) had graduated from FSU. The next thing you know, the guy was posing him a question regarding his relation to Florida State. Dick, now into his second can of beer, took off on this theme like a rocket.

Dick: "Man, I'd never been to Tallahassee before, so many hills. In fact, I'd never been on the FSU campus, and I was amazed at how *serious* they took the game. When I arrived late that Friday evening of my visit, I meandered around the campus looking for a friend, having no idea of where his dorm was. Well, I accidentally ended up at a girls' dorm---I couldn't believe, as I was wearing a jacket with Gator colors, how warmly I was received by a bevy of young ladies, eager to be of aid in orienting me correctly, an experience completely *unknown* in Gainesville. And then, get this, in the middle of campus there was a large crowed of students surrounding a guy beating a big tom-tom. I was told that the drum had been continuously beaten for 24 hours *all week long!*"

The Guy: "Yeah, as I remember it, the whole school was excited. FSU had never won against Florida, and, having a dynamite team in Tensi-Biletnikoff, well, they were ready for a show-down in Doak Campbell Stadium. Tickets for the big game were as rare as gold."

Dick: "You said it. I spent Friday night at my brother's house. He had just started at FSU, coming up from Central Florida Junior College. Boy, was he ever giving it to me! The Seminoles were gonna thrash the Gators for sure, no doubt about it. The Tensi-Biletnikoff duo couldn't be contained, just you wait and see. We also have a tough, tough defense. So, how do ya like *them* apples!"

The Guy: "And what was your reply?"

Dick: "To be truthful, I was slowly starting to get the jitters. Seeing the tremendous support of the students, knowing that FSU had soundly beaten Kentucky, a team which had been ranked #5 nationally. Well, I was a bit apprehensive to say the least."

Asking if Dick would like a fresh beer, the guy walked off, leaving Dick alone with his thoughts. Now in his element, he started chucking shit around, enjoying the conversation, the warm ambience of the late, lazy afternoon.

The Guy (returning with a beer): "Tell me about the game. How did you see it?"

Dick: "Terrible. Tensi and Biletnikoff were too much. Never could get to Tensi really, the offensive line was too good."

The Guy (inquisitively): "... and the defense? Couldn't Spurrier move the ball?"

Dick (angrily): "Hell no. Every time we got near the goal line the damn FSU defense would stiffen. Spurrier was sacked by that damned linebacker, er, whatever his name was..."

The Guy (ingeniously): "You mean Jack Shinholser?"

Dick: "Yeah, that's the guy. Damn him, caused a Gator fumble at the goal line!"

The Guy (smiling): "Yeah, I remember that too, because I'm that Jack Schinholser."

A long pause ensued. Dick, dumbfounded, couldn't believe it. Here he was sitting all the time across from the famous Florida State linebacker (with the nickname "The Wrecker"), who, that evening, didn't seem particularly scary at all. Somewhat larger than Dick, but not impressively so. So *this* was the killer linebacker. In a much more subdued tone, Dick continued the conversation in a mixture of admiration, coated with a modicum of genuine atonement.

Dick (contritely): "... er, uh, sorry if I sounded a bit harsh in my comments, I, uh, didn't know who you were."

Shinholser (laughing): "No problem. I don't take football that serious anymore."

Leaning back in his chair, Jack began reminiscing about his life as a football player for FSU back in the mid-sixties, telling some hilarious tales about Pete Petersen, the football coach. Coach Pete was known for his ongoing series of malapropisms such as:

"I'm the football coach here and don't you remember it!"

"You guys line up in groups of three and then line up in a circle."

"Don't forget, I'm the head football."

While Dick marveled at these gems of humor, Jack finished up by telling him that after one of the players decided that pre-season practice was too tough, quitting the team, Coach Pete called all the others together, announcing in a dark mood of foreboding: "If any of you also are thinking of quitting this team, let me tell you something. If you quit this football program, do you know where you'll end up? In the *state penitentiary!*" Complete silence engulfed the room, with no one sure how to take this unexpected warning. Jack smiled, saying "typical Coach Pete talk."

As Jack turned around to attend to his wife, Connie, who had been seriously injured in an automobile accident and wore a brace, walking with a cane, Dick slid over to the other side of the room to talk with some more of Bob's guests, who were in the midst of praising Bob's new house. After adding his perfunctory admiration of Bob's skill, he then grabbed another beer and sat over by a window watching the late afternoon sky with its myriad of light-colored clouds.

With the subdued conversations beginning to lull him into a trance-like state, he reminisced over those events which had taken place some fifteen years ago. All four, Dick, Al, Bob H. and Bob E. had decided to do some spelunking in north-central Florida, driving up on a clear cool Saturday morning in Bob's black VW. Going under the name of the "Clique", they were, in a way, truly the *fantastic four* with Bob H. already explaining to the others how he planned to move up to Gainesville next year and attend high school there his senior year so as to best work on an upcoming project for the coming State Science Fair next year (where he would later earn the First Place award). Not to be topped, Al had just received a letter confirming his admission to the University of Florida for the next Fall semester (that spring he was awarded the Bausch & Lob prize for physics). Relaxed in the driver's seat, Bob E. said would he just wait until next year before making any major decisions. (Bob would score an incredible 490 points out of a possible 495 on the Florida State Senior Test, placing him practically in the category of half-genius!). Rag-tagging along, Dick, repeating his senior year, was facing two years of military duty beginning in just six months. Proud to be associated with such stellar individuals, he hoped he could keep pace with his buddies, all of whom were doomed to success in that glorious future waiting them in the sixties.

But fate intervened, with things evolving much differently than Dick could have ever imagined; Bob S. now dead (having taken innocent victims with him), Al somewhere out in Colorado playing the hippie, Bob E. working at various odd jobs in the Tallahassee area. No, this was definitely *not* the path he had envisioned for them fifteen years ago. And here he was himself, working in a state prison out in stultifying Jackson County, smack dab in the middle of the God-forsaken Florida panhandle, rudderless, dead in the water. If one thing redounded to Bob E.'s benefit, it was a strange, also symbiotic relationship with Dick's father. Whenever in Winter Haven, Bob would drop by for a long chat at 144, getting a real kick off talking to his father. This, however, was not so unusual when one considered that Bob had grown up without a father and, perhaps for that reason, thought Dick's father *to be authentic, true blue* – enjoying the *straight* talk his father employed, for with Cliff Mann there were no if, and, or buts. No fancy verbal footwork, only a hard, straight right to the face. What you saw was what you got. At any rate, Dick thanked his lucky stars that Bob always made an effort to help his father, also in the coming years of declining health.

What was that for a wonderful, wafting aroma which awakened him the next morning. Bob, up early, was cooking a humungous breakfast: eggs, bacon, sausage, biscuits – the whole works. Over the meal Dick had a chance to get to know Bob's girlfriend better; a pert woman who worked at one of many states agencies in the capital. She seemed well-grounded, intelligent and good for Bob, who needed a caring, stabile character around him. After breakfast the threesome took a walk around the outside of the house where Bob and Allyson had planted some crops just some six weeks ago, with the first young, tender sprouts beginning to show. Both told Dick they were really becoming knowledgable regarding raising vegetables, thus making themselves as independent as possible in that area. Keeping his thoughts to himself, Dick followed the two around the plot of land, thinking that both Bob and Allyson were classic examples of the 70's, with its *back to the earth* movement.

By the end of May, going to work Monday morning no longer meant steeling his nerves for a confrontation with recalcitrant inmates, but with him now concentrating on various students, who had made it obvious that they were ready to accept his aid in preparing themselves for the GED. Long gone were the verbal chastisements for misbehavior, with him only occasionally having to use the worst form of punishment – the banning of an inmate out into the insufferable heat of the plaza, where they would sit silently, an inert mass of wretchedness, with Dick's eagle eye on them. Now that the "bad weeds" had been spaded out, there was more time for real teaching, one-on-one advising, experiments (for the two upper levels), with Dick gradually learning more about the backgrounds of certain students and why they had come into conflict with the law, resulting in their imprisonment. Out of these encounters there developed a slow, but growing trust between him and certain inmates, a feeling that they could be relied on to do the right thing. Occasionally he'd hear faintly in the background the slight click from the loudspeaker up on the wall behind his desk. Pleased as punch with the calmness prevailing within the classroom, he was immensely proud of the changes he had wrought since taking over the class last January, when, to those listening surreptitiously in the office, it must have sounded much as if they had unexpectedly tuned in to a monkey farm, with all the loud jabbering going on, despite all efforts of the teacher to reach a modicum of peace and quiet so necessary for all inmates, were they to advance in their studies. Yes, it had certainly taken five unpleasant months of unbroken effort to gain the upper hand, but now he felt safely in control of things, ready to plunge ahead to new frontiers.

The news had been broached to him months ago, something he had expected for a long time. His youngest brother, Dan, was planning to marry his girl friend, Betty Gee, right after graduation from FSU. Winsome and blessed with an unbelievable talent for math (which had helped pull Dan's young ass through statistic courses) she appeared like a solide partner for Dan's goal of soon beginning a career in banking. Having chosen an auspicious date for their wedding, June 21st, the summer solstice, they had invited a score of friends and relatives to attend the ceremonies, For some arcane reason, which remained a mystery to Dick, Dan requested that all this brothers appear in tuxedos. *Tuxedos*! Those were fighting words for his brother, who, at this phase in his life, detested all forms of *bourgeoise snobbery*. Yuk, did this ever go against the grain of his political beliefs. Ugh. But it was family, and he knew instantly he would have to silently submit to this, well, insult to his ideals. Whatever the origin of this moral turpitude, he realized immediately that resistance would be seen as pure egoism on his part, a cruel slight to his brother and future bride. So he didn't try to fight city hall, just role with the punches, put on a happy face and make sure his brother had a wonderful wedding.

As luck would have it, the day before the wedding in Tallahassee saw Doug and Dick accompany their father driving over to a shop in order to pick up the tuxedos which had been rented for two days. Sitting up front, Dick absent minded fiddled around with the car radio, trying to find a decent station. Doug ensconced in the back, was checking the address of the shop they were looking for, thus, except for the tweet-tweet, whirl-whirl of Dick's dialing, everything was still. Unable to find any music he liked, Dick turned off the radio, leaning back in his seat, regarding the street ahead of him. When they appeared within his view, walking nonchalantly along the sidewalk on the left side of the road, Dick instantaneously thought to himself – uh oh, the worst possible scenario! For there, in broad daylight, strolled a carefree pair of young adults, possibly students, a *black* man with a *white* woman! Quickly Dick, trying his best to turn his Dad's attention away from the approaching couple, uttered something completely asinine statement such as:

Dick (much too loud): "Look, over there, to the right! Can't you see that…that…"

Doug (unaware): "What are you talking about? I don't see anything."

Dick (desperately): "Over there, to the right! Can't you…"

All in vain. Too late. It was as if a volcano had suddenly erupted, a verbal Vesuvius spewing red-hot lava in all directions.

The father (enraged): "Goddammit, would you look at *that!* Right in public, a goddamned nigger with a white women! Here in the middle of town! This is what you get from forcing integration on the South! Hellfire, this is what your goddamned civil rights crap has led to!"

Stunned by this outburst Dick remained silent. How should he react? As the apex of the eruption had been seemingly reached, he heard a strange sound, a sort of humming coming from Doug in the back.

Doug: "Dum-dee-dum, dum-dee-dum. La-dee-dee, la-dee-dee."

In a split-second Dick grasped what Doug intended in initiating this nonsensical tune – what a stroke of genius! In the past year such an outburst by their father would have caused an immediate counter-attack by his sons, ranting and raving about how could one hold such old-South, racist prejudices, speak in such denigrating terms over other human beings. Of course, in doing that, they were merely stoking the conflict into further heights. Doug, intuitively rejecting a further continuation of this no-win situation, trod a whole new path – instead of fighting their father, he chose to simply ignore him, not letting himself get baited emotionally.

Dick (picking up on this): "Oh, what wonderful weather for the wedding today. Why this is perfect for taking pictures too. Luckily I've got two roles of film."

Doug (grining): "Dum-dee-dum. La-dee-da, la-dee-da."

Obviously frustrated, their father began to sputter, swiftly losing steam, realizing that his sons were tuning him out, offering a passive resistance to which he was defenseless. Through sheer serendipity Doug and Dick had discovered *the* answer to years of fruitless arguing – just simply ignore their father, making it clear that they no longer took him seriously.

Resplendent, not a bad word at all to describe the bride as her husband gently placed the gold ring on her finger. While family members and friends were snapping pictures like mad, Dick, after a few pro forma shots, faded off to one side, while the large white wedding cake was ceremoniously cut. Well, he thought, three down and two to go, seeing as Dave had married in '69, Doug in '72 and now Dan in '75. However, try as he might, he saw little chance that either he or Jim would be taking the vows anytime in the near future. Jim's present relation was rocky, whereas Dick was strictly out in left field, with no girl in sight – anywhere! No one was later quite sure who had the idea, if nevertheless it seemed cool at the time. With Dave, Jim and Doug getting down on their knees, Dick and Dan climbed on their backs, while their Mom was hoisted by two strong men up on top of the pile, forming a kind of rough pyramid, with some wag calling them the "Pyramid Pips".

The next day saw Dan and Betty loading their car, ready to drive down to Miami, where Dan was to start his new job at the Flagship Bank. When Dick asked Dan why he kept referring to the car as the "Duckmobile", he was told that Dan had inadvertently flooded the whole truck while washing the car, a minor mishap, jokingly leading to the car's nickname. Even though they were going way down to Miami, they'd also be close to Fort Lauderdale where Dave and Marylin were working, so the whole Mann family would still be together in the Sunshine State.

Excelsior!

A s the summer progressed, so did his relations with the inmates, him now having more time to talk to them individually, to pose questions far beyond the narrow confines of classroom texts, seeking to sneak a peek behind their normal demeanor, thus also discovering just what unholy skein of events had led to their incarceration, seeing as they were so awfully young, almost all between 18 and 22, including a handful of 17 year olds. Later, when Dick attempted to assemble this jigsaw puzzle of assorted lives-gone- wrong, one thing in particular was striking. If he had heard this once, he had heard it already a hundred times – the plaintive voice of inmates sadly moaning "if I had only listened to my Mom (or my wife, or my girlfriend)." Their backgrounds differed greatly, from the rural farmland Panhandle, speckled with small towns, down to heavily populated Dade county encompassing Greater Miami. Of course, you also had a number from central Florida too, especially the Tampa/St. Pete area, then, sliding up I-4, Lakeland, Orlando and Daytona Beach. After months of stealthy observation he was amazed at the wide spectrum of personalities, defying any hopes of dividing them into simple, easily understood categories. Some, exuding an unbelievable, seemingly inexhaustible *joie de vivre,* literally lit up the classroom with their entrance, while others carried their own personal dark-cloud, hovering over their heads, withdrawn and sullen. There were the jokers, always ready with a fast quip, and those so volatile that one had to constantly be on the alert to avoid an explosion. The small group which caused him the most personal anguish consisted of those persons so obviously in need of psychological treatment, who instead, were here locked up in a prison! So, the question was simply "was tun?" Fully aware of the limitations involved in any feeble attempts at changing the world outside his classroom, Dick decided to make an even greater effort to raise the knowledge and insights of the young men placed under his auspices, under his *responsibility*. Here, tucked away beside the Chattahoochee River, deep in the Panhandle's armpit, he was now on his own, far away from those academic circles espousing the theories of *Mitbestimmung* and democratic socialism, he would have to stand on his own, attempting to create, be it merely within his own classroom, a better, more egalitarian world, in which he could excrete, if only to a small degree, his influence in awaking the political and social consciousness of those young men entrusted to him – and thus he set out to do just that.

That very evening, snug in his room sitting at his spacious desk, he gazed fondly at the collage of posters on the wall beside him which he had collected abroad, particularly those from Germany, reminding him pleasantly of days past. Under the bright orange *JUSOS in der SPD* poster, a large black and white photo of Salvador Allende. Up above a small poster announcing the showing at the Bali Kino of the film *Kühle Wampe oder Wem gehört die Welt*. On the left side of the desk a bitter-sharp lithograph by Daumier. Over on the far wall a large poster of Alexander Dubček with the words *Svoboda – Suverenita – Socialismus – Demokracie*. Beside it hung a long role of calligraphy by the famous Chinese poet from the T'ang Dynasty 杜甫 (Du Fu):

朱门酒肉臭,路有冻死骨

荣枯咫尺异,惆怅难再述

Translated into English it read:

Behind the red-painted doors, wine turns sour, and meat stinks;

On the road lie corpses of people frozen to death,

On the battlefield there are white bones!

A hairs-breadth divides opulence from dire penury,

Drawing power from this thirteen hundred year old opprobrium, Dick, who had purchased a sheet of white cardboard paper late that afternoon, began cutting out one foot squares, then, with the aid of a red highlighter, drew the first of two sayings in Chinese characters. The first, aimed at invigorating the inmates to see learning as a life-long endeavor, said: 活到老,学到老 (live until old, learn until old), whereas the second was more political in content, stating one should: 为人民服务 (serve the people). Before class the next morning, he posted them above the green board for all to see, curious as to the response of the inmates – would they even notice? As for the administration, well, they should actually be proud of him, attempting to really motivate his students, stress academic progress as a good thing in itself.

For weeks on end he had been wrestling with the same question, namely how to join the academic classroom teaching with the inmates on-the-job training since Monday through Friday, when they weren't in class, they were out working on a construction project beyond the education compound. A pragmatist at heart, plus a true believer in combining *Theorie und Praxis*, Dick was determined to go beyond text book world of classroom teaching, attempting instead, to find a workable program of also offering the inmates knowledge which they could not only apply on the construction site, but later in everyday life i.e., in a future occupation. So, one hot, sweaty afternoon, while the cleaning crew was swabbing down the room, he lit off for the construction site, convinced that the workers and supervisors would be glad to see him, willing to aid him in his attempt to implement a true *praxis-oriented* mode of teaching. The closer he came to the site, the more confident his gait became, with him literally stomping along, head held high awaiting the first signs of recognition. Well, he didn't have to wait long before hearing catcalls from up on scaffold.

Inmate: "Hey, Mr. Mann, whut you doin' over here?"

"Look over there, why it's Mr. Mann. Whut you be doin' here?"

Dick (jauntily): "Oh, just checkin' up on you guys. Wanna see if you're really working and not just sloughing off."

Inmate (laughing): "No, we done be working. Sho' nuff. That's on the ups."

Right in the middle of this convivial conversation there suddenly appeared a red-haired, burly supervisor, striding swiftly toward Dick, his face twisted into a scowl, indicating immediate trouble, which was not long in coming.

Supervisor (grimly): "Who *are* you?!"

Before Dick could eke out a reply, the man continued.

Supervisor: "What the hell are you doing over *here*? Who gave you permission?"

Dick, now clearly on the defense, stuttered out a reply, hoping, somehow it would be understood and gratefully received by the interlocutor.

Dick: "I, er, I'm the new science teacher over at the education compound and…"

Supervisor (interrupting): "And what in the hell are you doing over *here*?!"

Dick (timidly): "I'm trying to find out what the inmates need, I mean, trying to combine what I teach in class with that which they apply practically, you know, in their vocational training."

Supervisor (perplexed): "What the hell are you trying to say?"

Dick: "You know, solving problems with pounds and ounces, basic chemistry, the fundamental laws of electricity and ..."

Supervisor (exasperated): "No, I *don't* know! And you can move your smart ass right out of here. You have absolutely *no business* here on the construction site. So you can get the hell outa here right now!"

Abruptly turning on his heels, the man walked away leaving Dick alone.

Dejectedly, Dick trudged back to the education compound, slinking into his classroom like a beaten dog. Bitter as he was, he had to grudgingly admit that he had pulled a boner. Sure, in retrospect the supervisor, as crude as he may have been in his treatment of Dick, was right. Dick should have gone to Mr. Sexton and explained his case, asking permission to visit the site well in advance of his action. Moreover, he hadn't reckoned with this much resistance, with people not the least interested in his idealistic goals, his great leap forward in initiating new pedagogical methods at ACI.

As if wanting to underscore his malfeasance, driving a final nail into his coffin of great expectations, he was cited to the front office the next day where Mr. Sexton gave him a real dressing down. What did he have in mind going over to the construction site on his own hook? Didn't he realize that he was working in a *prison*? Did he think that every employee could just decide for themselves, regardless of prison rules and regulations? Stricken impotent by this avalanche of criticism, Dick was merely able to nod silently in agreement, proffering an occasional "you're right", hoping to mitigate this brutal chastisement. Upon leaving the office, he felt the verbal lashing he had just received by no means commensurate with the misdeed he had committed, the action in itself having been so well-intended. Six months ago he was locked in a struggle with the inmates, now, or so it seemed to him, after having succeeded in restoring an atmosphere conducive to learning, he was facing an intransient foe in the administration itself! My Lord, was today just a foretaste of things to come?

Two days later, one of the inmates finally noticed the Chinese characters above the green board and, pointing upward, asked Dick, "what it wuz?" Not wanting to go into too much detail, Dick replied briefly that those were words of wisdom in Chinese, taking the time, however, to explain the meaning. After lunch one of his better students also queried him as to why he had chosen to use Chinese? Once again, Dick interpreted the characters one by one, this time going into more detail, mentioning the fact that he had spent some fifteen months on Taiwan. This news spread among the inmates like wildfire, with one asking him if he knew other foreign languages. Being frank, he answered that he had also studied Russian for two semesters, adding of course, that he was merely able to speak in a limited manner, possessing a vocabulary of around one hundred words at the most. One thing led to another, with an inmate inquiring if Dick would be so kind as to print the Russian alphabet on the green board. Seeing that this was an advanced class which obviously showed interest, Dick busied himself listing the following letters on the left side of the green board: а б в г д е ж з и...etc. Then, acceding to popular demand, he wrote a few words, phrases in cyrillic, such as:

Как деда? Хорошо сегодна, спасибо.
(How are you? Good today, thanks.)

Я американец. Вы русский человек.
(I'm an American. You are a Russian.)

До свидания, мой друг.
(Goodbye, my friend.)

Originally this was supposed to be a one off, a short break in the academic routine, however, as he soon discovered, he had unintentionally started a major firestorm, with this phenomenon spreading through the classes for days on end. Although he thought he had made it absolutely clear on the first day that English and Russian were, of course, separate languages, many of the students failed to grasp this and started writing letters to their parents and friends, simply using cyrillic letters in place of english ones in the full belief that they were writing Russian! Weeks later inmates were still receiving letters from home, full of amazement regarding their son's attainment. When he attempted to erase the alphabet und phrases from the green board he was met with a storm of dismay. He dare not in any manner besmirch their starlit hour. Нет – no way!

To be exact, it occurred exactly two days after his thirty-third birthday on July 17th and, how could it have been otherwise, it was completely bereft of any warning. Right in middle of his fourth period, with the class still, concentrated on their classwork, the door suddenly opened to reveal a group of unexpected visitors, obviously some kind official visit, but from whom? Leading the group into the classroom, Mr. Sexton, pointing at Dick, announced to all that "here is our science teacher, who just joined us recently, but is really doing a bang-up job." Then moving around Dick's desk, he introduced him to the Lieutenant

Governor of the State of Florida, J.H. Williams. Seeking the proper words, Dick shook the hand extended, mumbling a few perfunctory phrases to "Jim", who scanned the room quickly, seemingly trying to acquire an overall view of the lay of the land. All went well until "Jim" spotted something highly unusual in the background, to be more specific, the Russian alphabet and phrases, now suddenly having gained a powerful, even threatening political importance.

"Jim": "What, what is that on the blackboard over there?"

Mr. Sexton, now wide-awake, sensing some latent threat, spun towards Dick, his eyes narrowing, mouth twitching.

Mr. Sexton: "Ahem, well I do declare. I'll guess we'll have to ask young science teacher, I'm sure he has *some* kind of an explanation, right Mr. Mann?"

Dick (hesitatingly): "Er, well, as a matter of fact, it's Russian."

"Jim" (surprised and shocked): "*Russian?* Why in the world should you be teaching inmates Russian?"

Dick could see Mr. Sexton flinch, completely stunned, unable to answer the query, he, turned, asking Dick to please explain to everyone as to why he had written all these *Russki* phrases on the green board?

All heads in the room shifted around to peer at Dick, wondering how he could credibly respond to this hot potato of a question. He himself was dumbfounded. How could he possibly extricate himself from this trap? Actually one which he had unknowingly set himself. With lightning speed his cerebral neurons desperately sought an answer to the question posed. Then, literally at the very last moment where it seemed that all was lost, the solution came to him in flash.

Dick (calmly, almost condescendingly): "Excuse me, but aren't you all aware of the importance of today's event?"

Dead silence filled the room.

"Jim": "I don't understand. What event?"

Mr. Sexton (peeved): "Speak clearly. What event, what are you talking about?"

Having psychologically carefully set up his ten pins, Dick now sent his ball sailing down the alley.

Dick (proudly): "Today the world will witness an *historic* event. For the first time, an American Apollo space ship will rendezvous and dock with a Russian Soyuz space craft – a scientific milestone! Why President Ford himself is going to call the Astronauts and Cosmonauts and congratulate them. Moreover, they'll be docked together for two *whole* day, conducting *scientific* experiments, communicating in both Russian and English! Now this is a splendid example of détente in action; *both* countries cooperating in space *for the benefit of all mankind.* That's why you see Russian written up there on the green board. Any questions?"

"Jim" (a bit embarrassed): "My gosh, I'd forgotten all about it. You're absolutely right, this is truly an *historic* event! Mr. Sexton, you should be proud to have such farsighted, inquisitive teacher. I wish we had more of these kind of persons working for the state."

Mr. Sexton (now smiling broadly): "Yes, believe you me, I know how lucky we are to have such extremely qualified personnel such as Mr. Mann teaching at this institution."

"Jim" (shaking Dick's hand): "Thanks for all the hard work you put into your task. It's people like you who are helping these inmates not only pass their GED test, but also learn more about the world outside of prison - seeing that Cape Canaveral plays such an important role in Florida. Best of luck to you."

As the group left the room Dick could hear Mr. Sexton chortle some final remarks about ACI really being *up to date*. The inmates all took it in stride, not overly impressed by the visitor, but grateful for the interruption. No one, except Dick himself, realized how close he had come to going over the abyss, he and his hare-brained idea of writing the Russian alphabet and phrases on the green board. Luckily some fast thinking on his part had him avoid the worst, transform a possible disaster into a shining victory. Still, he began to realize on what thin ice he was skating, reminding himself to be more careful in the future.

Some two weeks later, on the way to work, he heard on the 7:30 news that the former boss of the Teamsters unions, Jimmy Hoffa, had disappeared, leaving no trace. Dick had read Bobby Kennedy's book, *The Enemy Within*, back in high school, in which the Teamsters union had been criticized as corrupt, Mafia infested. While Dave Beck had been described as the major target of the government investigation, his sidekick, Jimmy Hoffa, saw the trials as a vendetta, not only against the union, but also as a personal crusade against him personally, led by President Kennedy's younger brother. Both men had a series of run-ins with one another, both refusing to back down. Excited by the book, Dick, always a tad over-eager, drove over to Lakeland on his own hook, determined to smoke out the local Teamsters leader. Young, inexperienced and ill-prepared, he simply made a fool of himself, with the older union leaders laughing at him for his lack of knowledge of the local union, taunting him for that what he was – a rather ignorant high school boy, in way over his head. Now, fifteen years later, Dick figured, as did most of the media, that having lost his control over the Teamsters due to a long prison sentence, Hoffa was trying to bulldoze his way back into a leadership position, one which the Mafia was presently satisfied with. And, being the Mafia, they had decided to take care of the intruder in their own sweet way.

A Brief Respite

Although his job was a good deal for him financially, with Dick finally having a positive cash-flow, it also meant leading a life far from the centers of culture, with little to attract him outside of an occasional drive over to Tallahassee for the weekend and spending the night at Doug's house. Otherwise there was nothing to do except work on his Chinese, read a book or watch television. Each week he'd purchase a copy of TV Guide, glance through the upcoming week, circling the programs which seemed of interest. For the most part there were, perhaps, three or four circles a week, usually documentaries or old films shown on Friday or Saturday evenings. Sometimes, the programs he tuned into were of such poor quality that he simply turned off the TV set, not willing to waste his time on the junk shown. However, there were books readily available; thus he spent much of his spare time reading, trying to catch up with an America which he'd been neglecting for the past eight years. One book in particular gained his attention, the title of which he'd heard in various conversation among his cohorts in the last few months. The book was entitled "Deliverance", describing the adventures of four middle-aged men from Atlanta, who decided on the spur of the moment to canoe down the Nantahala River in northern Georgia, wanting to add more spunk in the lives, get back to nature, relive those days of being carefree young men. Aptly said, the men soon found themselves *in over their heads*, a theme which seem to hold an irresistible attraction to Dick, having experienced a similar situation himself and also having seen it happen to countless other young men – including close friends.

As a consequence, Dick was intrigued when Jim and Doug suggested that he accompany them and three other friends on a kayaking trip along the upper Nantahala toward the end of July. It would only be for a long weekend, driving straight up through Georgia, kayaking, then returning home. His brothers, however, made one thing in particular abundantly clear from the start; if he were to come along on the trip, he had to learn the famed "Eskimo roll". As to Dick's query as to what this might entail, the answer came with explanation. If one were to capsize, especially in rough, white-water, there existed two solutions; one either chose an often panicky exit, literally bailing out of the kayak, risking taking heavy shots from rocks and boulders, having to swim to shore, arriving soaking wet, minus one's kayak and paddle! Bad scene. Or, if one had mastered the "Eskimo roll", one could, with a few deft flicks of his paddle, right the kayak in a jiffy, continuing placidly downstream much as if nothing major had really occurred.

Brother Dave, who had flown up from Ft. Lauderdale in his blue and white Cessna to visit some friends in Tally, even offered to teach him the technique necessary by borrowing Doug's kayak and using a friend's swimming pool. While all the Mann boys had learned to steer a canoe through their camping trips with the Explorer scouts, Dave stressed to Dick that, unfortunately, this was *not* the same thing – not by a long shot. Nevertheless, the technique itself was rather simple – hell, the Eskimos had been doing this for thousands of years! So there was no reason why his brother couldn't master it, right? Damn right.

After lugging the kayak over to the swimming pool, Dave, in his bathing suit, hopped in, paddle in both hands, beaming confidently at his brother sitting at the pool's edge, and commenced to demonstrate his skill with fervor. Deliberately he capsized the kayak, which for some seconds lay dead in the water. Then, the paddle, as if guided by some mysterious mechanism, appeared, breaking the water's surface, the flat edge now parallel to the water. With one powerful downward *swish* of the paddle the kayak popped up to display a grinning older brother, who, not satisfied with a solo effort, kept repeating it again and again, almost spinning around like a top. With a few strokes Dave reached the side of the pool, indicating it was now Dick's turn to learn this new skill, which, in all honesty, was actually *very simple*. Right?

As he slipped into the kayak Dick felt a modicum of confidence, seeing as he had little problem in keeping the craft stable in the water. Hmmm, he thought, sort of similar to a canoe. Dave then jumped into the pool, grabbing the bow of the kayak, stating that he would be there to right Dick if he should have initial trouble mastering the roll, which, inherently, was *not very complex*. After receiving the high sign from Dick, signaling that he was ready, Dave flipped the kayak over, sending Dick into the deep. Now under water, Dick found that he had completely lost his orientation, no longer exactly sure where the surface lay. His first, furtive attempts to right the kayak were lamentable, with his paddle hardly breaking the surface, forcing Dave, with a mighty heave, to once more right the craft, revealing a soaked brother, rattled and spitting out water. Hardly had he come to his senses then Dick heard his brother tell him to really concentrate, as once more the kayak was flipped over, again plunging him headfirst into the water. This scenario repeated itself several times, until Dave, showing leniency, suggested taking a break, wanting to talk things over. While Dave went inside to get a cold Coke for his brother, Dick tried vainly to grasp what he was doing incorrectly, having merely been able to muster a few, feeble attempts at righting his craft. The basic problem was that of orientation, with him not able to discern exactly in which direction he should aim his paddle. He made an effort to image his position under water, coming to the conclusion that his body was extended *too deep*. Perhaps he should bend forward, practically resting his head on the kayak itself, this would bring him in a better position to break the surface with his paddle. This seemed promising.

Only taking two or three shorts slugs of Coke from the bottle, he told his brother that he was ready for another go at it, adding that he now had a solution to the problem of lack of orientation. With a thin smile of agreement, Dave once more placed himself at the kayak's bow, letting Dick slip into his seat. When flipped over, Dick immediately place his head firmly on the hull ahead of him, reaching out to his left, with the paddle held as high as he could, then, with a powerful pull, the kayak spun on its axis, with Dick popping up in the pool like a cork! Wow! Dave marveled, Dick too. After three or four more tests, Dave said they should call it a day, that Dick had truly mastered the "Eskimo roll" and had done it in grand fashion. Just like his other brothers he had shown that he *had the right stuff*.

Evidently his brothers, in wise foresight, realizing that Dick's skills were basically at the novice level, chose a calmer river for their fledgeling brother, with rapids merely in the number 2 level, with a few 3's thrown in to provide at least a modicum of adventure. None of them, excepting Doug, had ever been schooled in kayaking, so it was truly the better part of wisdom not to try and tackle something like the Natahala, which was really over everyone's head. Sharing a car with Doug, the latter regaled him with stories from his job at the Florida Retirement Department, where his boss kept admonishing his staff to keep a low profile – *don't make any waves*. Moreover, his brother had been diving in the Chipola River recently and, get this, had the luck of finding some real Indian *arrow heads*! This sort of gave Dick a small case of the green envies since he (and many other kids) had dreamed of something like this during their Boy Scout camping trips. This being Dick's first trip all the way up to the Georgia – North Carolina border, he was amazed at the sheer length of the state – the equivalent of driving all the way from Jacksonville down to Ft. Lauderdale! As the conversation slowly dried up, Dick reflected on the last couple of years, realizing that his brothers were all now entering mid-life, getting married, settling down, having jobs, thus gaining a certain stability. Yep, all except one, and this thought never quite disappeared, following him like a shadow, although, for the most part, he successfully repressed it, more or less keeping it in permanent abeyance.

Indeed the Little Tennessee turned out to be the perfect choice, not too difficult to master, but also having some sneaky rapids which could flip you over in an instant if you weren't paying attention. Unexpectedly, Dick, in his lack of experience found the water exceptionally cold, with him taking all measures to avoid capsizing. Thusly he paddled like walking on eggs, not charging ahead, but rather watching his brothers to see how they dealt with the tricky currents, trying to learn from their mistakes. He saw Dave almost go under, able to right himself at the last moment. Later, when they had paused for a break, Dave said that the water sloshing down on his chest was so cold that he stopped breathing for a few seconds! Other kayakers along the river had their own individual problems, mostly caused by a lack of basic skills, in this context meaning that many, when they "turned turtle" couldn't perform an Eskimo roll, therefore having to bail out of their craft and swim ashore as best as they could – later standing on shore like a wet poodle.

Since the whole trip lasted only two days, they were a bit pressed to finish up by around two o'clock Sunday afternoon, so they started off promptly the next morning, only planning a break around noon. Stopping for lunch at the confluence of the river with a much smaller stream, they discovered they were not alone. Two other groups were also there, the one consisting of four young ladies, obviously locals. The other group made itself heard by an ongoing argument, which immediately seized the attention of the four brothers. Much to his surprise, Dick discovered that James Dickey's book, plus the following Hollywood filming, had caused broad ripples of interest in the Natahala River throughout the Southeast. A slightly obese, obstinate woman, who seemed to possess only minimal skills, sat defiantly in her kayak, while other group members attempted to dissuade her from her plans. The woman was *tout feu, tout flamme* that the group follow her down the Natahala the next day, not willing to admit that, with her lack of ability, she would be endangering not only herself, but the whole group as well. As if to underline this, two of the young ladies from the other group paddled by, heading up the shallow mountain stream, where the water was merely *two feet deep*. Their strokes were swift and deft, bringing them easily on up the stream. Well, thought Dick impetuously, huh, if they can do it, I can too! Hopping into his kayak he started to follow the two girls, who, some fifty yards upstream, had begun doing little tricks, suddenly pivoting their kayaks around, 180°s in one, swift motion. Meanwhile Dick found the going tediously difficult, him hardly able to get a decent stroke with his paddle in the very shallow water (not to mention the oncoming current). Now breaking into a sweat, Dick cursed a blue streak, suddenly becoming aware that the young women were observing him, obviously delighting in his predicament. Nonetheless, try as he may, he was only able, with the greatest of effort, to struggle some thirty yards upstream before the two young lassies barreled past him on their way back down, their paddles just flicking the water lightly. Piqued by this dent in his masculine pride, he sat quietly munching his lunch, thinking, oh well, there could be worse things. And there were.

The car towing the kayak trailer had been parked on the banks of Lake Fontana, so the plan was simply to follow the Little Tennessee to where it emptied into the lake – in itself, a well calculated plan. Unfortunately, two things had been left out of consideration. First off, the rather swift current simply disappeared when they entered the broad lake; secondly (even worse) the water level was extremely low, at times less than three feet in depth, making deep, powerful strokes impossible, meaning one had to extend the paddles further out, tiring and providing less thrust.

Sweating like a pig in his life jacket, he was told that the car and trailer was about a mile and a half away, meaning at least another half an hour of torture under the hot Georgia sun, paddling through the flat, currentless, brown-reddish soup. No one spoke, all bent forward in their kayaks, arms aching, rivers of sweat pouring down their faces. Strangely enough, though exhausted, on the long drive back through Georgia one spoke about the *real adventure* they had experienced and their willingness to undertake such a trip again.

Nouvel Terrain

Although, when astronomically seen, the days were already growing shorter, they seemed longer, even hotter. His Mom, sorely missing her native Pennsylvania, used to go into a rant and rave at that time of the year. Those outbursts always began in the weeks following his birthday. "Oh, she'd mutter in dark tones, they're here again, those damn long, hot and humid dog days!" A part and parcel of Florida, the panhandle also suffered through these torrid weeks. Now that he and Lawton were driving to work together, each one using his car for one week at time, Dick found his black plastic steering wheel practically untouchable when going out to the parking lot being as the AC unit took a while to cool the car interior. Upon driving out of the lot, he'd just barely touch the steering wheel, handling it like the proverbial hot potato. Luckily, the classrooms were air-conditioned, not as much as he would have preferred, but enough to keep the room temperature around 20°C. Now particularly, his favorite form of punishment for maleficent inmates proved especially effective – sitting alone on that concrete bank in the blazing sun worked wonders in aiding the students swiftly gain insights as to what they had done wrong, now ready to repent, their resistance melting like wax.

However, this treatment was applied much less frequently than months before since the relationships between Dick and the bulk of the inmates had reached the level of a guarded friendship, with the teacher, bit by bit, discovering the various backgrounds of his students, in some cases even slowly developing an empathy with them – hardly any of them being incarcerated for any heinous crimes. One needn't be a sociologist to quickly ascertain their socio-economic roots, their family history, education (or lack thereof). As for their transgressions, well, despite the wide spectrum of inmates, their reasons for being imprisoned could be easily short-listed: Theft, drug dealing, assault & battery, armed robbery. Many of his black students never had a father at home - if they did, it was not some one to emulate. In all his time at ACI, Dick only found *one* inmate who he considered upper middle-class - a good-looking black inmate from Gainesville, Florida, where Dick had spent four years as a college student!

Still basking in the warm afterglow of Lyndon Johnson's landslide victory late that fall, having been the Vice-President of the Young Democrats on the University of Florida campus, he liked to think that he too had been an active cog in that historic campaign. Working part-time and thoroughly tied up with his spring trimester courses, he still well-remembered the assassination of Malcolm X in New York as being a side-event, not particularly arousing any special emotions on his part since, hell, Malcolm had been gunned down by his own black Muslims, obviously carrying out the orders of Elijah Muhammad, the leader of the Nation of Islam, with whom Malcolm was on the outs. Moreover, much to Dick's distaste, shortly after the assassination of President Kennedy, Malcolm stated indirectly, but clearly, that JFK death was simply the result of "the chickens are coming home to roost". Adding to this, Dick had conversed with some young, black Muslims on Times Square back in the summer of 1964 while working at the World's Fair, surprised to find them demanding the same system of *segregation* as the KKK down south. Needless to say, this accounted for his disparaging remarks upon hearing the news on the radio of Malcolm's demise, figuring that this was merely one political radical less - or so he thought at the time. Years later, however, he discovered that the real reason behind the struggle with Elijah Muhammed was based on a pilgrimage that Malcolm had undertaken to Mecca, where he experienced an epiphany leading in turn to a rejection of the "white devil" doctrine he had espoused beforehand, now becoming more engaged toward a dialog between the races, calling for more understanding and cooperation, while, of course, demanding respect and equal rights for black people. Thus it didn't come as a complete surprise to yet discover a small, but active, group of believers in Malcolm among his inmates, a fact which he found out through a growing number of conversations with various black inmates, with them holding on to a whole heterogeneous mixture of beliefs, some with a grain of truth, others so farfetched that Dick marveled at their ability to assume some such arcane creed without questioning the source.

That summer reminded him of a wide, placid lake, where only occasional squalls would disturb the otherwise tranquil classroom world of his. Seeing as the stern stick of past months was so seldom applied, he now was able to offer the carrots in the form of some small experiments and, perhaps more important, beginning to show certain selected films to the inmates. He began with a simple, human-interest ones. For example, a film about Jane Goodall and her experiences in living with gorillas in central Africa – for the inmates a completely new world. The following film, however, was right down his own alley. A film by the National Geographic Society called *Dr. Leakey and the Dawn of Man*, a story concerning Louis Leakey and his wife Mary, who were archaeologists in eastern Africa in the 1960's, having discovered the bones of a pre-human creature they named *homo habilus* (the toolmaker) in the Olduvai Gorge in Tanzania, with Leakey estimating the age of the bones at approximately 2 million years old. Of course Dick underlined all this by drawing a rough map of the area up on the green board, emphasizing the fact that this was still further concrete proof of Darwin's theory about the origins of human beings as a species. Furthermore, he explained to the inmates how these *homo sapiens*, over time, began migrating in waves, beyond Africa into the Middle East, then on up into Europe and toward modern day India and China. Since the film was 60 minutes long there was no time to answer any questions.

The next day, however, in the middle of class, Stokely, a black inmate, who always seemed so self-possessed, strode up to Dick's desk, initiating the following conversation:

Dick: "Well, Stokely, what's up, need some help?"

Stokely: "I've got a few questions regarding the film we saw yesterday."

Dick: "O.K., shoot. What's on your mind?"

Stokely: "What I want to know is this: Was the film on the ups?"

Dick (smiling): "You mean you want to know if the contents of the film were correct, honest? Right? You wanna make sure nobody's givin' you the *double-shuffle?*"

Stokely: "Right. The film said we descended from the apes. Now do you think that's true?"

Dick (hesitatingly): "Well, to be more exact, it was trying to add more evidence to Darwin's theory that human beings *did* basically descend from ape-like creatures...but of course, millions of years ago."

Stokely: "So what you're saying is – the Bible is wrong. That we didn't descend from Adam and Eve. Right?"

Dick (chosing his words carefully): "Although the Bible might contain many words of wisdom, it is not based on modern scientific research, which is, as much as possible, trying to lend credence to a well-known anthropological theory."

Stokely: "So, you're still saying that the Bible is wrong!"

Dick: "No, I'm just maintaining that I think there's more *scientific* proof supporting Darwin's theory, that's all."

In the meantime the class had become all ears, everyone eager to see how this unexpected conversation played out. Had their teacher taken on the Holy Bible? Does he really believe in Darwin and that we are distant cousins to the apes?

Stokely (now very concentrated): "So, if everything you said is true, then human beings all actually come from *Africa*! Right?"

Dick (after a slight pause): "Yep, one can say that we're all of African origin, having left the continent about a million years or so, spreading out all over the globe."

Stokely (grinning broadly): "Hot damn! I knew Malcolm was right all along when he wrote that blacks are 'the original people of the world.'"

Dick (a bit sheepishly): "Well, at least anthropologically. I mean, if you want to put it literally, Africa is the birthplace of the human race."

Rows of stunned faces stared at him. Particularly the white inmates. Meanwhile Dick wondered how long it would be until the administration called him into the front office for a real dressing down, asking him just what the hell was teaching these inmates!?

The classroom toilet represented finally one place where inmates felt truly alone, able to go on their own during the classroom period without asking for permission. Although the toilet was nominally used for disposing of human waste, at ACI it served as a billboard, with inmates writing all sorts of comments, most being of a scatological nature, a trusted and true thermometer of the emotional atmosphere at the institution. It was here where many white inmates disclosed their feelings and thoughts which they would be afraid to do openly. During one of his checks during the first few weeks, Dick discovered that someone had written in large letters on the toilet wall: If black is beautiful, then I just shit a masterpiece! He considered scrubbing down all the walls, but realized, to keep the toilet free of graffiti he would have to interrupt his work each time someone went to the toilet; perhaps it would be wiser to let the walls serve as safety valve for pent up emotions. Sometimes he also wondered about which inmates had written the more sulfurous comments, thinking that no microscope had ever been invented which could look inside the human soul.

In his informal conversations with a handful of black inmates he could tell that, for the most part, they all seemed autodidacts, having snapped up bits and pieces of information here and there, vainly attempting to form them into some sort of understandable form which would give them a certain amount of intellectual stability, while also adding to their own credibility among other inmates. Understandably hot on Malcolm X, the small group appeared cool toward the non-violence stance of Martin Luther King (see where it got him!). Their big idol was, who else, the reigning world champion Muhammad Ali. Joe Frazier, respected as a boxer, failed to have that special flair, with Ali possessing true charisma, with the inmates awaiting the upcoming match between the two in October.

Meanwhile, Dick received a double blow-back from the front office, being told that the films recently shown to the inmates had precious little to do with the upcoming GED test, thus those types of films were no longer to be shown – only those directly connected to his science course. Secondly, and quite harsher was the run-in with Mr. Sexton toward the end of August. Dick, having returned from a weekend in Tallahassee, was accosted by his boss out on the plaza:

Mr. Sexton (disgruntled): "Mr. Mann, you ought to immediately get a haircut, your hair is too long!"

Dick (surprised): "But Mr. Sexton, I *just* had it cut this weekend in Tallahassee."

Mr. Sexton /adamant): "Now don't give me that old routine. When you signed up to teach at this institution you agreed to abide by the rules and regulations, right?"

Dick: "Yes I did. But I *just had it cut*. Look, it's still above my ears and, in the back, well, it's not touching my collar...yet."

Mr. Sexton (sternly): "Now let me tell you something Mr. Mann. Everyone at ACI must follow the grooming rules set down in the contract. We make no exceptions...not for you or anybody else."

Dick (pleading): "But I just had it cut."

Mr. Sexton (steamed up): "No use trying to weasel out of this. You signed the contract, remember? Now are you going to follow my demand?"

Dick (stalling for time): "Well, I'm *not* having it cut *immediately*. That's for sure."

Mr. Sexton: "Well, I'm warning you of the consequences. I'll give you one week to comply with the rules and regulations here, otherwise I'll have to insist on a special evaluation concerning your employment. I hope I've made myself clear."

Dick: "Well, I'll have it cut, but on a need to basis - when I consider it too long. I'll look in the mirror each day, then decide."

Mr. Sexton (scornfully): "Then let's hope it's within the next 7 days!"

The last months had seen him so involved in bringing a modicum of order and discipline in his classes that, excepting an occasional weekend in Tallahassee, he had little time for anything else, thus it gladdened him greatly when his older brother asked him if he were interested in meeting a girl down in Panama City, seeing as Jim had worked there and thus had a friend there who was willing to set Dick up with a date on the next weekend, that is, if he were interested. Despite his initial skepticism he agreed, knowing full well that the lay of the land in Jackson County told him his chances there were close to zero. Consequently he found himself hopping into his Kharmann Ghia one bright Saturday morning, driving along highway 231 through the flat, pine-studded countryside of the southern panhandle, mildly curious as to what awaited him down on the Gulf coast.

The young girl, Susan, was in her mid-twenties, about 5' 4", brown hair and slim body, also curious about the background of the guy she had been setup with for a date. Being that the weather was so gorgeous they decided to head for the sea shore, walking barefoot along the white, sandy beach. Having grown up in that city and working at a local real estate office, she began reeling off data about her home town much as if Dick were intent upon buying property there. As their trajectory carried them further down the beach, Dick began slowly tuning her out, his eyes now scanning the buildings to his left, mostly motels, restaurants and small businesses, all crowded along the edge of the beach, less than a hundred yards distant. Noting especially the shallow slope of the beach, Dick thought to himself that, should a strong hurricane ever strike this area that there would be hell to pay since the buildings were so awful close to the water. The further they walked, the more concerned he became, remembering fifteen years ago the damage that hurricane Donna had wrought in slamming the Keys and then barreling right up the gut of central Florida, even pasting his inland home town of Winter Haven with gusts of up to 132 mph.

Sensing that Dick's silence had become deafening, Susan suggested that they visit her tennis club, with Dick faking a great interest. Once at the club he was introduced to a number of members, all good friends of Susan, all of which seemed so similar in their stylish tennis shirts and shorts, all mid-thirtyish, tanned, invariably optimistic, with slight interest in this outsider Susan had brought along for the afternoon. Seldom had he ever felt himself so extraordinarily out-of-place – almost as if he were a left-wing Democrat stuck in a Republican stronghold. Susan ordered Cokes and pretzels and they sat down at a table with two other friends who had just finished a bracing game of tennis as the conversation meandered around through the usual series of themes, with inflation climbing to almost 10%, nation-wide unemployment peaking at 9%, while the latest blockbuster film "Jaws" constituted the most important subject of the day, with everyone praying that something like that would never occur off their own beach – My God, the tourists! As the afternoon waned Dick signaled that he had better hit the road back to Marianna, with Susan and friends concurring, probably happy to see this strange guest, with his odd stories of prison life starting to grate on the nerves of his captive listeners. On the ride back, Dick moaned and groaned over the bad hand fate had dealt him, with he himself at fault. He should have known better than to drive all the way down to Panama City on some wild goose chase like this, thinking that he might just hit the jackpot, when just by using common sense anyone could have told Bogart in advance that he was merely chasing a will-o'-the-wisp here in the middle of the year 1975. Of course once home he conflated the facts a bit in order to make his brother feel as if he had truly done a good deed; so while Jim visited a friend that evening, Dick picked up the TV guide to see if it had any solace to offer and it did. The late movie that evening was no less than "Casablanca", a film his Mom had raved about, with him chasing after the elusive butterfly, never able to catch it. Alone, lonely, the movie had a powerful impact on him, exactly the kind of film that suited his present situation and mood; Rick in Casablanca, Morocco and Dick in Mariana, Florida, both in a self-chosen exile, the two men having lost the woman in their lives.

Monday morning, Mr. Sexton cited Dick to the front office excoriating him for not following his demands and jabbing a sheet of paper in his hand, told him tersely that should he ever consider a job with the state, that "this document would be in his files *forever.*" Slowly walking back to his classroom Dick read the letter warning him of a pending investigation regarding further employment at ACI:

September 8, 1975

Mr. Richard Mann, Classroom Teacher II
Apalachee Correctional Institution
P. O. Box 699
Sneads, Fla. 32460
RE: GROOMING RULES AND REGULATIONS

Dear Mr. Mann:

In regards to our conservation of September 2, 1975 pertaining to the rules and regulations of this institution concerning grooming. At this time, I advised you that abiding by the grooming code was conditional on your employment. You assured me that you would abide by the rules and be in full compliance by Monday, September 8, 1975.

You failed to comply with this, so I am officially informing you that I am requesting a special evaluation pertaining to your employment at this institution.

Sincerely yours,

GARRIE CURLEE, SUPERINTENDENT

J. B. Sexton
Educational Supervisor

JBS: ah

Cc: Mr. Curlee, Superintendent
Mr. Owens, Personnel Manager

Seeking some method of retaliation against this hassling from above, he finally found a solution to his problem – a color film concerning cancer. He had received a secret, hot tip from some one working in the library that the film, a rather harmless half-hour documentary, had some short, but gangbuster scenes, with the worker filling Dick in on all the details. Correspondingly, in the middle of the week Dick closed the window curtains, letting the film roll along to the click-clack tone of the projector. Mundane as such films are wont to be, the inmates lay their heads on their desks, some half- asleep, all wondering why their teacher, usually on the ball, had foisted this film upon them. Twenty minutes later came the scene Dick had been waiting for; a black-haired, comely young woman arrived at a doctor's office for a yearly check-up, where she was politely requested to disrobe her upper body in order to have her breasts checked for the formation of suspicious nodules. Talk about sheer cacophony, unchained emotions, a barge of boggy-woggy! Thunderstruck by scene they were watching, the inmates, roared, howled, beat their desktops, stamped their feet tumultuously – a scene of unbridled passion! Afterward, wanting to avoid anyone snitching, Dick warned them to "hold it down", "keep their cool", lest he be forbidden to show such films in the future. Obviously they took it seriously since he didn't hear anything from the administration. Another first-down and ten to go.

In late August a teaching assistant was added to the staff in the form of a young man fresh out of the University of Florida, who grew up near Orlando and majored in English. Joe DeChristofara rather closely resembled one of his boyhood scoutmasters only smaller - an inch shorter than Dick, 10 pounds lighter and possessing a pale visage. Joe also reminded him of his brother Dan, in always being so chipper, so open, so friendly. Of course, it certainly didn't further hinder their growing friendship that Joe happened to be Catholic – more so than Dick, but by no means really dead serious about religion. One final aspect that fused them together was sports, with Joe a real basketball freak; with Dick, although preferring football, fully enjoying playing the hoop game too. Unfortunately, Joe too had run into stiff resistance from Mr. Sexton on account of his naive, liberal attitude. For example, curious to expand his knowledge of the ACI system, he talked one of the black secretaries into accompanying him on a visit to the famous West Unit, a small compound where the "lifers" were incarcerated. Unknown to Joe, this was a strict no-go area, one reason being that "lifers" were considered extremely dangerous, liable to unexpectedly strike out at prison personnel at the slightest unintended slight, basically having nothing to lose. Boy did Joe get a verbal tanning from Mr. Sexton for putting himself *and* the young lady in danger! Joe himself thought the chewing out was caused by the fact that he had dared ask a *black* woman to accompany him. Having been raised in a rather sheltered environment, Joe was shocked by the redneck attitudes he encountered at the institute, with Dick silently thinking "welcome to the club". Joe's presence also made lunch time more palatable than before, since the teaching staff tended to sit at the same tables. Occasionally he was able to talk some black women, working in the administration section, to come over and dine at the teacher's table, a taboo break which led to lively conversations.

A Mystery Within an Enigma

Busy grading a paper he scarcely noticed the classroom door opening, lost in his thoughts, probably thinking it was the clean-up crew returning early from their smoke break. Not until he heard the shuffling of the feet approaching his desk did he glance toward his left, surprised by what he saw. Three black inmates standing some feet from him, all silent, waiting for Dick to speak. One of the two smaller inmates was a student of his, the other probably from over on the low side. However, it was the man in the middle who grabbed his attention, a stolid form over six feet tall, muscular, seemingly chiseled out of pure anthracite, topped off by a handsome, proud face. Curious, Dick blandly asked the visitors as to why they had come to see him, did they have any questions? The big man answered first, speaking in a clear, uncluttered English, lacking any trace of a southern dialect, his eyes directly focused on Dick's own.

Big Man: "I was told that you showed a film confirming that man originated in Africa, right? At least that's what some of the brothers affirmed."

Dick: "Yes, I showed them a film supporting Darwin's theory."

Big Man: "Am I correct in assuming that you too believe that humans first developed in eastern Africa?"

Stunned by the measured English, the even tone, the polished pronunciation, Dick quickly sought to find out just who this fellow was. How could a person of this obviously well-educated background be doing time here in prison? Who was this young man, who was capable of expressing himself so cogently?

Dick: "Well, all the scientific proof up until now seems to support the theory that humans spread out from the African continent throughout the world. So, I'm not an expert in that field, I just know what I glean from books, films, magazines."

Silence.

Dick: "If you don't mind me asking, I'd like to know who you are and where you're from?"

Big Man: "My name is Clarence and I'm from the Chicago area."

Low Side Acolyte (piping up): "He done be somebody who knows another guy who said he knew Malcolm X!"

High Side Acolyte (chiming in): "He be the real thing!"

Dick: "What I'd like to know is this where did you go to school?"

Clarence (trace of a smile): "I went to a Catholic school, St. Pauls, where the nuns were as tough as nails, but they *did teach me*. We even read some Langston Hughes my senior year. Ever heard of *I, Too, Sing America* or *Let America Be America Again*?"

High Side Acolyte (sneering): "Well, have you?"

Dick (embarrassed): "Er, uh, for example I know he's connected to the Harlem Renaissance…"

Clarence (decidedly): "But you haven't read any of his poems, am I correct?"

Dick (somewhat contritely): "No, I haven't."

Desperate for a convincing answer, Dick racked his brain to come up with a credible reply, regain parity with Clarence. Five long seconds later he did.

Dick (tentatively): "Did you ever heard of Jean Toomer? I remember a few lines from his poem *The Blue Meridian*, they go like this:

'Islanders, newly come upon the continents,
If to live against annihilation, ...'

(stumbles)

'Must outgrow clan, class, color...'"

Then he added something about, "the symbol of Universal Man."

Clarence: "No, I haven't, but it sounds good."

Low Side Acolyte: "Ask him about that pork, Clarence."

Clarence: "Mr. Mann, I believe you are aware that both Muslims and Jews abhor pork and for a good reason, for pigs are dirty, filthy creatures. By the way I've been informed that you take a different stance. May I ask why?"

Dick (cautiously): "From a strictly scientific standpoint I see nothing inherently wrong with eating pork – as long as it's properly cooked. Now I agree that it's not a good move to eat pork raw or undercooked."

High Side Acolyte: "No, pork is swine – dirty and dangerous!"

Dick (firmly): "No, it's not the pork itself, but rather *trichinosis* that's the real danger."

Low Side Acolyte (puzzled): "Whut?"

Clarence (with disdain): "You're just doing that science jive. The Koran forbids pork, the Bible too. Take Levitius. Isaiah or many others. And you're telling me it's *not* unhealthy? You and your white science; you probably believe that those astronauts really landed on the moon, right? While the black community knows it all took place in a TV studio."

Now this really took the cake! He had just gone through a series of hassles with the administration, then along comes a Black Muslim to dress him down for teaching the basic principles of natural science. With the distinct feeling that any attempt at a further constructive conversation had already ended, Dick concluded with the following argument.

Dick: "Look, both the Bible and Koran were written well over a thousand years ago, with little exact proof of who wrote them. Moreover, they've been translated several times into various languages. Natural science is based on laws that are the result of repeated experiments. These laws hold true until they're proven to be incorrect by new, repeatable evidence. Our modern life style is based on this, get it?"

Silence.

His gaze fixed on Clarence, Dick remembered what another inmate had said about the former's shining black skin. The inmate had intimated that the man's skin was of such a coal-black that a slight aura of blue radiated from it. Now carefully perusing the inmate's arms, Dick thought he really could indeed perceive a slight shade of indigo. Or was his imagination playing tricks on him?

Clarence: "You're wasting your time with your white science. There are other spiritual laws man must obey; thus we follow the teachings of the late Elijah Muhammad. You and your worldly learning have little to say to us."

Upon uttering these words, he pivoted on his heels, walking swiftly out of the room, his two acolytes dutifully following him, almost colliding with the returning cleaning crew whose eyes widened in seeing the three black inmates, the crew extremely curious as to what had just transpired, with Dick keeping mum as King Tut, merely acknowledging that a short talk had taken place. Furthermore, he decided to keep the incident private, not to inform the administration nor anyone else, including the teachers, since he didn't consider the opinions expressed in anyway a threat to anyone in particular nor the institution itself. On the other hand, he was forced to admit the limitations of his own goals because they often had little influence on the inmates coming from completely different backgrounds than his own. News of the attempted assassination of President Ford out in California didn't cause the slightest stir among the prison's inmates, who had more important things to concentrate on, their EOS (end of sentence) for example. That alone had become their alpha and omega, their paramount goal.

An Unusual Hiatus

S ome three weeks before, he had received a letter from Tim Currey inviting him up to New Jersey for his graduation ceremony at Seton Hall, where Tim had earned his Master's in Far Eastern Studies. Nice guy that he was, he offered free room and board at his parent's house, not so far away from the campus in South Orange. Seeking a break from the last six months of tedious work, Dick decided to take a full week off, fly up to New York, go over to Tim's for two days, then spend three days up in Boston, a town full of pleasant memories. In 1955 the whole Mann family had gone on a four- week vacation up the East Coast to Pennsylvania, all seven persons crammed into a light-blue four-door Ford Fairlaine, not forgetting to visit Uncle Hap in Bean Town. In 1962, Dick had enjoyed a one-day liberty in Boston as a sailor on the USS Enterprise. Money was no problem since over the the last seven months he had been assiduously saving coins, so that he could easily afford the trip.

Tim Currey had roomed with Dick and another young Chinese guy on Taiwan back in 1973-74, after Tim had received his Bachelor's degree. Dick found himself astounded that his roommate had deviated from studying Chinese, and had begun to learn the Mongolian language. *Mongolian*! Chinese in itself was considered, at that time, a bit strange, slightly off base, but *Mongolian*! Dick didn't know if he should praise Tim or chide him. When Dick asked him what he intended to do with the language, Tim laughed and replied that he had just applied for graduate school at Seton Hall, and as for work afterwards, well, he'd cross that bridge when he came to it. Dick himself not being so sure as to his long-term plans, cut Tim some slack, knowing how difficult it was to plan for the future, with hope many times grudgingly relenting to the demands of reality.

Arriving by bus from New York in the late afternoon he was met at the bus station by Tim, who drove him over to his parents house a few miles away, both good friends immediately jabbering away about their experiences on Taiwan. That evening, after a tasteful meal, sitting around the living room with a glass of wine in his hand, Dick, having, up till then, carefully tried to steer the conversation away from himself, was now cornered like a rat, with no exit, when Tim's parents politely inquired as to what he was doing in the States after his studies in Germany and on Taiwan. His honest, straight forward answer immediately served to throw a wet blanket over the conversation, with the parents expressing their regrets that such a fate had befallen their son's friend. Later, in the bedroom, Tim explained that his parents were also extremely anxious concerning his own future, also being well aware of the difficulties in minting a major in Mongolian into a future job. In being so candid, Dick had stoked the unrest of the parents to an even higher degree, although, of course, Tim knew Dick had not intended this. Thus not taking umbrage.

At first, slowly emerging from a deep, dreamless sleep, he couldn't ascertain exactly what it was that he heard, nor its source, only the longer he listened, the louder it became. To him it sounded more like some one trying to shift gears in a car, albeit with a faulty clutch so that the gears couldn't mesh. A terrible, metallic, grinding tone – almost screeching. It was a sound he had never heard before in his life. What could it be? Within seconds Dick succeeded in locating the source; it was coming from the bed beside him where Tim was sleeping, grinding his teeth ferociously! Now wide awake, Dick wondered if his roommate was perhaps having a horrible nightmare and should be awakened. Or maybe Dick should let him sleep on until the grinding phase passed. Unsure of what to do, he simply bided his time until, after some five minutes, the sound slowly subsided. Nevertheless, it took him a while to fall asleep again, wondering what could possibly be the root cause of this unusual unconscious behavior, conjecturing that it just might have to do with that evening's discussion – or might it have had different, deeper lying reasons? In the past he had heard about people, like Robert McNamara, the Secretary of Defense during the height of the Vietnam War, whose wife later reported being disturbed by her husband's grinding. Well, for Dick it was the first time... and he reverently hoped, the *last* time.

Graduation Day at the Seton Hall campus turned out to be a miniature version of that which he'd seen in Hollywood movies, with a crowded stage, music, caps and gowns plus a huge swarm of parents armed with everything from Kodak Brownies to movie cameras. With the sun shining on the event, the mood was festive with Dick being swept up along with the rest, as speeches were held, diplomas given, students hugged, photos made, all in all a joyous occasion. Afterwards, the whole Currey family had been invited next door for lunch by neighbors, an Italian family, which really went for broke in serving a delicious meal, including a fabulous lasagna. Then, when all were finished eating, something happened which Dick had never experienced. Families and friends just sat there conversing pleasantly, as if nailed to their chairs. Just about the time where Dick was getting yancy, ready to bolt into the living room, coffee/tea and cake were served, which, in turn, prolonged the meal even further, with Dick, now getting into the swing of things, was beginning to really enjoy finding himself, involved with one of Tim's high school friends who had spent some time with the US Army stationed in Germany. Topping things off, Tim invited Dick to come along to a private party held at a friend's house down in Keyport thrown by a group of graduating Seton Hall students, an invitation to which Dick gratefully agreed.

The house itself resembled a small mansion with a spacious garden in the rear, where some thirty young men and women were milling around drinking beer, wine and munching on finger food, just the relaxed atmosphere which allowed Dick to glide in grab a cold beer and mingle among the college grads. Right away he was introduced to a crowd of Tim's friends, many having heard of Dick through Tim's tales of his experiences on Taiwan. Now completely in his element, Dick regaled several guests with his many cultural miscues caused by his lack of knowledge as to Chinese customs and mores. He was halfway through his second beer when he felt someone tugging on his elbow. It was Tim, who told him to come quickly into the living room, where a group of people sat in a large parabola around a TV set. Tim told him to have a seat, that everyone was awaiting a new program on PBS entitled *Monty Python's Flying Circus*, asking if Dick had ever seen it. Surprised at the question, Dick replied honestly that he had absolutely no inkling whatsoever as to what the title even meant. *Monty Python's Flying Circus* sounded strictly off-the-wall, weird, strange, unusual. When told that it concerned a group of English satirists, his expectations of the unknown show plummeted even deeper. However, not wanting to be seen as spoilsport or killjoy, not daring to ruin the pleasant atmosphere, he just sipped on his beer, skeptically viewing the TV screen when the new show began. Within the space of a few minutes he found himself totally immersed in the program, roaring at the clever jokes, the biting satire, which fired vicious salvos in all directions, the whole 360° in which nothing was sacred or out of bounds. If fact, one skit was so uproariously funny that Dick actually laughed so hard that he fell off the couch, which, of course, provoked even more laughter. He hadn't seen anything like this since the days of Sid Caesar in the mid-fifties. This was good, this was hilarious! Unfortunately, there was little chance of receiving the program out in Jackson county, in the heart of the Florida panhandle.

That night as he lay in bed waiting with baited breath for the much feared *gnashing of teeth* to once again begin, he let the day pass in review, a wonderful day, with just one rather minor fault, one small smudge on his escutcheon, a minor wound to his ego which never seemed to heal: The graduation ceremony itself. During his own cap and gown ceremony for his high school graduation he felt curiously unrelated – why be excited when an F in Phys. Ed. had cost him a whole extra year of high school, graduating a whole year later, meaning he was clearly a year *en retard* of those classmates he had known since kindergarten. Adding insult to injury, a stupid mistake by his academic advisor years later at Gainesville had required him to tack on a summer semester in order to graduate, causing him to miss the graduation ceremony and merely being handed his BA in a small cardboard tube down the cool, brightly neon-lit basement of Tigert Hall. In Berlin, the very same act was again repeated, with him going up to the third floor of the institute for political science, where he was simply given an official-looking sheet of paper announcing his attainment of a Diplom (MA) in political science – end of story. It was in this morass of self-pity that he finally fell asleep.

Since the flight to Boston didn't leave La Guardia until the afternoon, that gave him time to wander over to Flushing Meadows to visit the former site of the World's Fair held in the summers of 1964-65. Seeking solace in the past, he was sorely disappointed to find merely remnants of those decade-old memories because the fair grounds seemed to have been swept clean excepting for the Unisphee and a few other buildings, the roads now empty, vacant on both sides. Strangely enough, he had little trouble in finding where both the British Lion Pub and the Berlin Pavillon once had stood since they were right across the street from the Singer Bowl, which sat empty, awaiting some possible future use. Standing roughly where the Berlin Pavillon used to be, he recollected that day on the Florida university campus when he, walking across the mall between classes, was given a handbill announcing that the Brass Rail restaurant chain in New York needed college kids as workers that coming summer, and since Dick's school was on the trimester system, this meant that he'd be free to work in mid-April. Despite the fact that he had not the faintest idea of housing, lacking any friends or contacts, Dick decided, against all odds, to sign up for a the summer job – not even sure how much he would be paid! What a fool! And yet this decision gave him an impetus which would, over time, propel him into a completely different trajectory than he, could have ever imagined that day in Gainesville, when he, in a burst of youthful enthusiasm, decided to cross the Rubicon, with all the risks, and work at the World's Fair – "and that had made all the difference."

His three day sojourn in Boston could be aptly summarized as a sort of *chercher le temps perdu* with him vainly attempting to find that innocuous office on Tremaine Street in Boston, where he had met Ted Kennedy when the latter was campaigning for the Senate, or meandering across the Havard campus mulling over the unexpected death of his uncle Hap at the young age of forty-two, a crushing blow to Dick's Mom. Hap was the golden boy of the family, first Pitt and then Harvard law school, all avenues open, blue sky ahead, or so it seemed. Of course the Liberty Trail was a must, along with the chance to see Marcel Marceau that very evening. On his final day in the city Dick decided that the one thing lacking was a tea cup, indeed a fine, porcelain one, similar to those which he had seen on Taiwan. That afternoon he finally ran across a shop selling china, which he quickly entered, gazing at the variety of porcelain dishes, vases, ornaments; amazed a this cornucopia of fine tableware. Watching Dick wander rather aimlessly through the story, the owner came out behind his counter, engaging Dick in the following conversation:

Owner (friendly): "Excuse me, may I be of help? Are you looking for something in particular?"

Dick: "Thanks, I'm looking for something rather simple. Just a tea cup... with a saucer of course. Something similar to that which I saw on Taiwan."

Owner: "Well, then, let's see what we have to offer."

Dick estimated the man to be around fifty something, six feet fall, slim, well-dressed and sporting a thin moustache. Obviously quite knowledgeable about far eastern culture in general, the owner went into detail about Chinese porcelain, explaining in depth the styles of the different dynasties, also informing him that the crux of the matter regarding tea cups could be found in the *thinness* of the material used, a fact that many buyers were, unfortunately, not aware of. Having chosen a cup and saucer under the Argus-eyed owner, Dick found that even after the purchase itself, the man seemed intent on continuing their conversation.

Owner (leaning over the counter a bit): "Please do tell me if I'm mistaken, but I thought I detected a slight southern accent on your part, so, am I right, are you from the south?"

Dick (smiling): "Yeah, you're right. I try and keep it under control, but having been raised in the south, well, there was a bit of collateral damage you might say."

Owner (quickly): "Oh no, I didn't mean to criticize your accent. Why I know some very fine people from the south, believe you me."

Dick: "Well, I'm happy to hear that. Occasionally we get a little *heat* from northerners- if you know what I mean."

Owner: "You know something, I completely agree with you. Let me tell you something – many of us fully agree with the attitude of you southerners. Particularly your resistance against those folks in Washington!"

Dick: "I'm sorry, I don't quite follow you."

Owner (banging a fist on the counter): "O.K., I'll put it more succinctly: We're fed up with this busing business, trying to integrate the schools with a sledgehammer, sending kids clear across Boston, leaving their neighborhoods just to mix the schools. Now what do you say about that!?"

Startled by the sudden shift in theme and tone, Dick was literally stymied as to what to say, not wanting to seem impolite, however, not in agreement with the man's stance. Thus he did his best to calm down the waves.

Dick (slowly, deliberately): "I agree with you on one thing. Busing is not a perfect solution."

Owner: "You're damned right it isn't! That's why it should be stopped - *now*!"

Dick (limply): "But, but do you have a viable alternative to it? If you don't bus, then the schools will remain segregated, and you don't want that, do you?"

Owner: "Listen, everything here was O.K. until they started that damn busing, going right over the heads of the local population! Now is that democracy? Those people down in Washington are cramming all this *down our throats*. Believe me, we're fed up with it!"

Sensing imminent defeat in the air, Dick attempt a strategic retreat, trying to allow both sides a chance to save face.

Dick: "Down south we're slowly solving this problem in our own way, step by step, so to speak. Black men are being elected into office as mayors, now even to Congress. I'll grant you it's slow and tedious work; however, we're gradually making progress and I'm sure you people up north want to keep in step with us, right? My point is – if busing doesn't work, then try something else. I'm sure with your tried and true liberal traditions you can find both an effective and equitable solution. Don't you think so?"

The owner, mouth twitching, now glaring at Dick as if looking at a turncoat, a traitor, nevertheless now unsure as to how best to respond to the last question without lowering the level of the conversation down to outright racist rant, doing his level best to somehow square the circle of an historical American dichotomy, the huge invisible, but palpable elephant crowding the room.

Owner: "O.K., you may have a point there. What I'm saying is, however, that busing is simply counter-productive - if you know what I mean. It's causing more problems than solving them. You just can't *force* wrong solutions on people, now can you?"

Quickly grabbing his package from the counter, Dick walked quickly out of the shop, while tossing a rather flippant remark over his shoulder about the importance of creating a true level playing field for *all* participants. On the flight back down to Atlanta, Dick considered the recent event just another nail in the coffin of youthful illusions. For years on end he had dutifully believed in the simplistic categories: right – wrong, true – false. black – white, even North – South. Having been raised among the open bigotry of so-called *southern* institutions, he tended to see the *North* as a counterweight, a righteous, moral instance. Hadn't the abolitionist movement begun in New England? Ergo, for him, the further north you went, the less prejudiced the people must be. Or so he thought. No, today was merely another example of that which he had experienced within the last fifteen years. Racism was truly omnipresent in the United States. What was it that "Rap" Brown said in the sixties about violence being as "American as cherry pie".

Upon his arrival back in Mariana, he was surprised to find a letter to him from Berlin; from the markings, some kind of important contents. Opening the envelop carefully he found it contained an announcement of an upcoming wedding involving two students whom Dick had been friends with at the *Studentendorf* in Berlin. Fredi and Bärbel had been a pair since 1970 so it was only common sense that they had decided to finally tie the knot. Somewhere in his files he had their telephone number, thus he decided to surprise them with a call shortly before the wedding, scheduled in late October.

Back in the Saddle Again

"Ridin' the range once more,
Totin' my old .44,
Where you sleep out every night,
And the only law is right,
I'm Back in the saddle again."
- Gene Autry

If there was one, single theme which seemed to dominate all others the last two weeks of September it had to be the upcoming bout between Joe Frazier und Muhammad Ali, the rubber match, which would finally prove which man the real champ, the best of two out of three. Among the black inmates a overwhelming majority were siding with Ali, the champion who had, with his famous "rope-a-dope" tactic, had been able to outbox, plus outthink George Foreman in Kinchasa back in 1973, in an historic upset seen world-wide on television. Moreover, here was the man who had been stripped of his title due to his unwillingness to fight in Vietnam ("I ain't got nothin' against them Congs") and converted to Islam. Clearly Ali represented the pride and respect of most black Americans. Of course there was also a small handful of "Smokin' Joe" supporters, many of which saw him as an underdog, indeed one who had been constantly denigrated by Ali himself, who kept up a steady barrage of epithets like calling him an "Uncle Tom", intimating that Joe was merely the "white man's champion" and, going further, demeaned him as looking like a gorilla. A few were aware that Frazier had a true working class background, having cut wood, done farm work and grown up in ghetto. Nonetheless, Ali danced, rhymed, and with his good looks and fast tongue was the gallant figure of the inmates.

While Dick possessed a firm belief in science coupled with a healthy distaste for rank superstition and hocus-pocus, doubts did appear in September, when a tropical storm by the name of Eloise nipped the edge of the Yucatan peninsula, heading in the direction of New Orleans. Then, as if pushed by some unknown cosmic force, began recurving to the east and strengthening in force into a class 3 hurricane. Although Marianna escaped with heavy rainfall and some gusty winds, poor Panama City got racked up good, as the storm made landfall between it and Fort Walton Beach. Much as Dick had calculated while walking along the shallow beach some six weeks before, considering the motels and restaurants having been constructed too close to the gulf should a powerful storm surge with high waves and winds ever hit the beach – exactly that happened that late September. The damage ran into the millions, scores of motels were simply washed away or severely battered by wind and waves, while Dick, safely ensconced over at ACI, felt somewhat guilty for having "foreseen" the looming threat to the beaches along the so-called Redneck Riviera. Weeks later, he and Jim drove over to survey the damage, Jim eager to see how Panama City (where he worked for three years) had survived the storm. That which they observed along the beach looked even more grisly than the photos they had seen in the local newspaper back in Mariana. Whole swathes of beach property completely vacant, the former buildings were now gone, leaving behind the concrete foundations among the white sand in the glowing sunshine. Upon leaving, Dick asked his brother if he thought the new buildings to be constructed would be more solid, built to better withstand wind and wave. Taking his time to think over the question posed, Jim answered "probably not".

In the meantime, Dick had decided to "go native" and began ordering various and sundry garments from Sears & Roebucks, from blue jeans, shirts, even a raunchy cowboy belt with big fake turquoise in the middle of the buckle, and all this along with his brightly checkered shirts plus his thick hair, just long enough to provoke second looks, not enough to demand another official reprimand. By this time he felt more and more like the Duke of Earl, confident that after so many difficult months, he was finally able to teach effectively, in synch with the inmates, while, at the same time, keep an unsteady truce with the administration. By the time late September had rolled around, Dick's had gradually morphed from that of merely being a teacher, into the role a *pater familias*, seeing to it that all of his students were treated equally according to their needs – bearing down on some, cutting others some slack, knowing the background of each inmate. When class began, he would not only check attendance, but also check them out physically to assess their conditions. It was in this very situation that he noticed one morning that one of his hispanic inmates by the name of Garcia, was sporting a big shiner, so Dick later called him up to the desk to find out more details:

Dick: "Say man, what happened to you? Looks like someone hit you with an ugly stick, right?"

Garcia (smiling slightly): "Yeah, I guess you could say that."

Dick: "Well, I hope to hell somebody else has that 'ugly stick look' too."

Garcia: "You can be sure he does."

Dick (smiling): "Good, glad to hear it. Now, what the hell happened?"

Garcia: "Nothin' particular. One of my buddies was being hassled, got into a fight, so's me 'n few brothers jumped in to help him. Simple as that."

Dick: "Who started it. Whose fault was it?"

Garcia (with a laugh): "Dunno...but I can tell you who finished it. Let's put it this way: you jump one off us, you jump *all* of us. *Comprendo?*"

Dick: "Si. All for one, one for all, right?"

Garcia: "If you want to put it that way, yeah. You push one of us around, you're pushing all of us. We stick together."

Dick: "That's real solidarity. (Then almost as an aside). Cesar Chevez would be proud of you."

Garcia (astounded): "You, you know Cesar Chevez?"

Dick (shrugging): "No, not really. But I've read a lot about him and how he organized the farm workers in California. Bobby Kennedy visited Chavez back in 1968 supporting a strike."

Garcia (clearly interested): "Do you have a book about this, about him?"

Dick: "No I don't. (Pause) But, if you're *really* interested, well, I could get you a copy. Not immediately, but I'll be working on it. O.K.?"

Garcia: "Si. And thanks a lot."

Dick: "De nada. Don't mention it."

His last words could both be understood simply as an empty phrase, or also be interpreted as a warning not *to spill the beans*, not to spread the word, but rather let the matter remain dormant, grow weeds, show great patience. In doing this, Dick realized he was sailing into uncharted waters, quite possibly endangering his employment at the institute plus perhaps also one of his own students. At any rate, Dick decided to drive over to Tally the next weekend to browse around the books stores next to the FSU campus, where he might just find the book he was looking for.

Three weeks before that, he and Jim had decided to attend the wedding of their cousin Frank Madden in Hollidaysburg, Pennsylvania on October 4th, correspondingly purchasing airline tickets for the flight from Tallahassee to Pittsburgh via Atlanta. Both brothers held a deep attachment to their northern relatives, much closer than the southern ones, and always dropped by "H-burg" when they got the chance. Happily, these feelings were reciprocated by the relatives, so that all felt a certain responsibility to keep the relationship fresh and strong. Jim, always stingy with his annual leave, had decided that they should leave on a Friday and return that Sunday, with him thus having to only spend one day of leave. Dick grudgingly agreed, actually rather having flown off on a Thursday. During the short weekend in Tally, he spent Friday and Saturday night in Doug's house, which was rather spacious and saved him money since he could cook for himself and, if he was good at one thing, it was saving money for some long-term goal – that having been taught to him by Dave, his oldest brother. Saturday afternoon saw Dick browsing through various books stores, when, lo' and behold, he chanced to run across a small, paperback about Cesar Chevez – exactly what he was looking for!

Seeing as Doug and Karen were out in the Panhandle at her father's house, leaving Dick alone, consequently he decided to take in a flic, finding *Give 'em Hell Harry!*, playing at a local theater, a movie about Harry S. Truman, starring James Whitemore. Arriving back home rather late, Dick showered, then dove into bed, ready to catch some zebras, when, perchance, he happened to glance down into a small gap between the bed and a large concrete block upon which a reading lamp stood. Yikes! What was *this*! There, in the hollow of the block lay – could it be? -it sure looked like, a *gun*! A medium-sized pistol. Fighting against his atavistic desire to reach down and grab it, his mind spun, seeking a reason for the hidden firearm. Now he was fully aware that there *had* been murders committed in Tallahassee in recent years; in fact, his brother Dave had considered it a wise move to even purchase a Colt .45, which he used to keep under his pillow in the 60's. One had to also take into account that a man *did* have the right to protect one's wife and property - now that was a *natural* fact. Of course, on the other hand, just having a gun itself could also been seen as a ticket to mayhem. One could be shot by the robber or, worse yet, one could end up shooting a friend or even member of the family by mistake! And, in the worst case scenario, what if, in a fit of anger... No; better double padlocks on the doors than a gun. In the back of his mind, he was wondering if Jim had a gun stowed away somewhere in the house on Decatur Street. Who knows, maybe Dan had one too. That would be more than fitting, he the odd-ball, the individualist *par excellence*, working unarmed in a prison and *even* at home! Such were the thoughts which accompanied him all the long drive back to Marianna.

Thursday morning classes knew but one theme: *The Thrilla in Manila*. Inmates marveled at the capacities of both fighters to absorb such punishment and still remain standing. Ali, with his comeback in the late rounds, was considered *the* champion for having taken Franzier's best, hardest shots without folding. A heap of praise to for Joe, who wanted to continue the bout although he was half blind! While most black inmates thought the fight sure to go down in boxing history, others were more skeptical, noting that both Ali and Joe were immediately brought to hospitals where they had to spend the night, having suffered such a beating. Listening to his students hoop and holler over the match, Dick dared to wonder if the fight hadn't actually symbolized that last big fight for both boxers since the damage to both had certainly shortened their careers accordingly, thus they would never quite be the fighters that they once were.

Return to the *Burg*

In April 1946, WW II having ended, the Mann family packed up their luggage and left their Mom's home town of Hollidaysburg, Pennsylvania, heading south along the eastern seaboard in the direction of Florida, where they were to set up shop in their father's native city, Winter Haven. The three older boys however, shared fond memories of those early years; thus, particularly emotionally, returning there was in a way returning to those halcyon childhood days once more. Perhaps more than the other brothers, they felt the greatest attachment. Whereas Jim and Dick quickly adapted to their new environment in Florida, their older brother, Dave, never seemed to have really overcome the feeling being *déraciner* against his will, leaving his favorite aunt plus his school friends. However, all of the brothers possessed a deep attachment to their relatives in H-burg and were always welcomed with open arms when they were able to drop by in later years. Consequently, Jim and Dick regaled each other with tales of their childhood adventures during the flight from Atlanta up to Pittsburgh.

At the rent-a-car counter, all went smoothly until paying for the vehicle. Jim, as usual, being extremely careful with his money (if not to say scrooge-like in his tendencies), wanted to pay the tab in cash, right up front. The salesman, however, declined this offer, explaining that he could only accept a credit card payment, thus the battle lines were drawn, both sides obviously not willing to back down. In working for the federal government for the past six years Jim had gained a lot of savvy in dealing with customers, knowing how best to handle difficult situations. Seeing as the line behind them was growing increasingly uneasy, with the people eager to get their car and drive off, Jim began berating the young man for not accepting a cash payment, repeating that he did not possess a credit card (which was not true)! Under duress, the salesman made a phone call to an upper office somewhere, with the answer coming down to just take the money and give the customer a car! On route to the Burg on highway 22, Jim drove with one hand on the wheel, the other gesticulating as to how he had forced the asinine agency into accepting cash, with Jim unwilling to hoist all his spending onto his credit card. A victory for all cautious consumers, as he put it. Soon they had passed by Nanty Glo, approaching the turn off to Gallitzin, the town where their Mom had been born some sixty-four years ago, a small town with a Polish background, ergo the name.

Heartedly greeted by their cousins, aunts and uncles, they managed to eat a quick snack before being told that Steve, Tom and company were taking them to a Friday night football game just a ten minute walk away at Hollidaysburg High School, their cousins' old alma mater. Dick, the inveterate football fan, queried his cousins as to tonight's opponent, whereby with one look at their fallen faces he knew that the question was a real bummer. Sure enough, Tom told them that tonight's opponent was none other than the highly ranked team from State College High School - coming from the same city as Penn State! Not only that, but they possessed a crushing running back by the name of Matt Suhey. When Dick tried to the make a joke out of the player's name by using the term pig-sooey, he failed miserably in gaining any laughs. A half an hour later Dick understood why no one had laughed. The big, burly State College line punched gaping holes in the Golden Tigers defense, allowing the powerful running backs to penetrate deep into the secondary. It all seemed so unfair, so one-sided, when Matt Suhey, a 5' 11", 215-pound fullback ran truck-like right over the smaller, 170-pound defensive backs. Shaking their heads in disbelief, Steve and Tom decided to call it a night early, leaving the game at halftime. Later that night, sitting around drinking beer, Steve began a rant diatribe against the US Army and the military in general, an outburst that astounded both Jim and Dick in its vitriol since both had been damn glad to get their military service behind them, but, on the other hand, didn't harbor half the animosity of their cousin. With their active duty with the US Navy long behind them, the Mann boys felt that their military duty was pretty much a mixed bag. Frankly admitting that they had gained much important experience during this period, plus saved a lot of cash for college, the whole thing could be seen as one big trade-off, with them basically having made altogether a good deal.

The next day offered Dick an unpleasant reality check. During a late breakfast, he happened to mention, more or less as an aside, that if it weren't for the wedding, well, it would be a good day to drive over to Pittsburgh to catch a Steelers game, a remark which was immediately met by loud guffaws from his cousins. When he asked why everyone was laughing, he was told that tickets to the Steeler games were as rare as hen's teeth, that the home games had been sold out at the beginning of the season. His uncle Earl summed things up with the pithy remark that, after all, professional football was a *business*, right? All at the breakfast table nodded their silent agreement.

Four months before, Dick had attended Dan's wedding and, in comparing the two, found a great deal of similarities – the clothes, family, church, music, even the speeches which all seemed to contain a skein of common banalities, surely well-meant, but nothing really radical or spontaneous, at least the way he saw it. Still, the convivial atmosphere of the party afterward added an extra luster to the afternoon, with there being no problem at all in finding a partner for interesting conversations. With the wine and beer allowing the tongues to loosen more and more, Dick soon discovered more small, unknown details concerning his family history, especially regarding his childhood days when his aunts were busy helping their sister with her four sons during the war, their father being down in Baltimore, working at an oil refinery, only able to visit his family now and then. Moreover, another nail was driven deeply into the coffin when he was told with abated breath that one of his relatives had the gall to vote for George Wallace back in the Presidential election of 1972! Now what did he have to say about that?! Nothing, as a matter of fact. This was merely further proof to him that ignorance abounded everywhere - even in Pennsylvania.

However, he hesitated to damn the Yankees unfairly because, since his childhood days, he had always had a certain minority complex vis-à-vis the north in general, and the big cities in specific. It seemed to him that literally *all* what he considered American cultural – books, movies, magazines, newspapers, TV shows, etc. - had had their origins in cities such as New York, Boston, Chicago or Los Angeles. In meeting people from these cultural centers he swiftly became aware of certain deficiencies regarding music, literature, history, foreign languages, blaming this lack of culture to his being raised in central Florida, a cultural backwater, in his mind. Sure Florida was catching up with the rest of the US, but still the innovative core lay clearly to the north, beyond the Mason-Dixon line.

As if to corroborate his suspicion, the band, which up to now had just provided a rather soft background music, promptly began playing a loud fanfare, tantamount to an important announcement. Without further ado, the band's leader grabbed the microphone, blurting out to the crowd: "Now we're going to do the hokey-pokey! Are you all ready?" The answer was a thunderous roar, mixed with applause. Pole-axed, Dick stared at the joyous faces around the table, thinking to himself "what the hell is this *hokey-pokey*?", finally finding enough nerve to ask the person sitting across from him. She gave him an incredulous look, as if he had just stumbled in from some godforsaken, podunk town way out in the boondocks. "*You've* never heard of the hokey-pokey," she said unbelievingly. Dick shook his hand. "No, I haven't," he mumbled. Smiling warmly, she said, "well, it goes like this:

You put your left foot in,
you put your left foot out,
you put your left foot in
and you shake it all about.
You do the hokey-pokey,
and you turn yourself around,
that's what it's all about."

She pulled him out on the dance floor, with them joining a large circle of participants who were lining up for the fun, including many of the small kids. In no time at all, Dick had grasp the essence of the dance, as the long list of body parts were called out one by one, with people, bouncing, spinning and gyrating, all laughing and singing, including Dick, who now felt fully in swing of things.

When Frank and his new wife later dropped by the table, Dick managed to steal the show briefly by asking the assembled if they knew why the newlyweds had chosen this historic day for their wedding? Silence reigned. Dick then added the punch line: "They obviously chose this precipitous, historic date for their wedding because today is also the 18th anniversary of the launching of the first earth satellite, the *Sputnik!*" Boy did that ever bring the down house. During the drive back to Pittsburgh he and Jim both agreed that they had made a wise decision in flying up for the wedding, keeping the family ties firmly in place.

The Nub of the Matter

T he week following his return rolled along placidly with the inmates studiously following the academic program and with no conflicts with the front office, all of which should have sufficed to fulfill Dick's wishes – should have, but didn't. Much too often he found himself mulling over the events of the past months, in particular Dan's wedding in June, plus the one last week in H-burg. If there were one undeniable fact, it was this: Dave, Doug and Dan were nuptially wed, and with Jim never at a loss for a girl friend. So here he was, alone in this godforsaken Panhandle, not only without a girl, but none in sight. Well, not quite. At lunch in July, he had sat vis-à-vis a new teacher, who it turned out was working over on the low side. A big woman, statuesque, about an inch taller than him, friendly, humorous and black. Brenda was her name. Gradually Dick found himself wandering over to the low side, in the morning before classes, during the lunch break or on his own afternoon break, always devising some reason for being there. Often, ten minutes before classes started at 8:00 am, they would find themselves involved in a harmless conversation, bantering, joking, enjoying each others company. Now and then, Dick would risk a joke that was a little risqué, so obviously *double-entendre* that she'd flash her broad mouth full of bright teeth at him, giving him a pleasant jolt. And then, with that good-natured, seemingly shocked look, reel out a long and deep throated "Mr. Maaaaaann!" Of course this was more than enough to start his day off on the right foot. He also knew that she lived outside of Marianna, in a small, black community and that she liked to go fishing. Many a time he had considered asking her for a date, always halting at the last minute, unsure of starting something he couldn't finish. Moreover, how would that look, some small, white guy with glasses beside this black Brunhilde? What would her parents say, not to mention the neighbors? Imagine if the word got out at ACI. No, he'd play his cards carefully, one day at a time, *auf Sicht fahren*, checking out the lay of the land far in advance.

One inexhaustible theme of conversations with Brenda concerned the varied treatment of the teachers by the inmates. Dick, over time, had noticed that most of the white teachers, be it men or women, were given a modicum of respect, which, however, had to be earned through instilling classroom discipline along with proving their academic competence. With the black teachers it was the same, excepting the black women. They were constantly given a rough time by the inmates, especially the black ones! In his talks with his inmates he had discovered, unfortunately, a wide-spread proclivity among his black inmates to use denigrating terms when speaking of women -whereby from the contents of the conversation, they were speaking about black women. He cringed at the derogatory remarks so casually dropped by these young men when they spoke of *bitches, whores, cunts,* as nonchalantly as if they were speaking about the weather in Jackson county or the price of rice in China. Brenda herself was often a target of such slights along with other black female employees.

A frank conversation he'd held with a small group of black inmates served to unexpectedly provide him with astounding new insights as to the experiences of many black (and possibly white) inmates concerning the treatment of women in general. One inmate had proudly told the group how he had dealt with a girl friend who had dared possess the audacity to contradict him in public, in front of his bros:

Inmate: "So's I showed her ass a thing or two. Just slapped the shit out of her, made her beg to stop. Showed her who's boss. Don't take no kind of back-talk from no woman."

Second inmate: "That's showin' her! Bust her lip when she's talkin' back to you."

Dick (taken aback): "That's, that's way you treat your girlfriends?"

Inmate: "The bitches gotta know where they belong, right?"

Second inmate: "Now you *know* that's right man!"

Dick: "Well, my oldest brother certainly wouldn't punch his wife. (Pause). You wanna know why?"

Inmate (curious): "Yeah, tell us. He be afraid she go' get a gun, right?"

Dick: "No, she'd go to police and press charges."

Second inmate (incredulous): "To the *po-lice*? Now how come she do that?"

Dick: "Next thing you know, she would have a lawyer and take my brother to court."

Inmate: "To court? For what?"

Dick: "He would be charged with assault and battery and, of course, she'd start filing for a divorce too."

Third inmate (breaking in): "Who's payin' for all this?"

Dick: "Well, should the judge find my brother guilty, then he has to pay! Plus move out of the house and get ready for a very costly divorce!"

Inmate (angry): "Damn bitch!"

Second inmate (laughing): "But she be laffin' all the way to the bank, right?"

Dick: "Well, don't forget, what I'm telling you is just theoretical, I mean, it *could* happen this way."

Inmate (caustically): "Yeah, *coulda* happened - in that honkey world."

Second inmate: "Well, that ain't gonna happen to me, 'cause I say fuck 'em, don't marry 'em!"

Third inmate: "Amen, brother."

Long after the three had left, Dick sat at his desk slowly digesting the gist of the harsch, misogynistic conversation, when the title of an old science fiction film from the early 50's popped into his mind - *When Worlds Collide*. Yes indeed, that film cogently summarized the polarized views of two completely different spheres of socialization and their resulting attitudes, toward women. Of course, it wasn't merely a black v. white scenario since it definitely crossed over racial lines too. Last week after classes, he went out to the parking lot to find that the ERA sticker on his car's rear bumper had been ripped off, with just a few ragged remnants dangling in the limpid air. Six months ago he would have had a temper tantrum, cursing at the cowardly perpetrators and the south in general. Today he just stood there, shaking his head quietly, now knowing that he should have expected this all the time, with such a sticker having a half-life measured in weeks in Jackson county.

The next Monday, he happened perchance to be sitting around after the lunch-break when Brenda walking by, dropped in for an informal chat.

144

When Dick insouciantly inquired about what she had done yesterday (thinking she'd been out fishing), she hesitated before answering his query. His curiosity now piqued, he awaited her reply. Brenda mentioned her father having held a small, special ceremony in honor of Claude Neal.

Dick: "Who?"

Brenda (a bit perturbed): "Claude Neal. Don't you know his name?"

Dick's mind scoured the long list of his present inmates, with no results.

Dick (blandly): "No, can't say I ever heard of him? (Pause) Should I?"

She gave him this glance - one which contained a touch of pity, joined with an almost patronizing superciliousness.

Brenda: "No, of course you couldn't know, you're not from here. White folks don't like to talk about these things nowadays. Do they?"

Sensing something ugly arising from a dark past, Dick nevertheless felt compelled to face the hard message he knew was in store.

Dick (tentatively): "No, they don't. (Pause). But I'm listening to you."

Brenda: "He was lynched right here in Jackson county. My father was a teen-ager back then in the 1930's; hell, he said it was *some spectacle*, my, oh, my. Hundreds of white folk came to see it, but they never gave him a trial, just cut him up, then strung him up – right in front of the courthouse in downtown Marianna."

Dick: "Did your father see this?"

Brenda (in burst of laughter): "Whut you say? Now my father wasn't plumb crazy, he knew when to lay low. That's common sense in the panhandle, 'cause the law sure ain't on *your* side – now is it?"

Dick: "I didn't realize it was so prevalent here back then. Was it mostly Jackson..."

She cut him off quickly, in mid-sentence, her eyes flashing.

Brenda: "Hell man, you're from Florida, where you been livin'?! Just go east of Tallahassee, there's a whole passle of counties – Taylor, Madison, Suwannee, Columbia, and it goes right down the middle of the state. You ever heard tell about Rosewood?"

Once again Dick dug deep into his brain, trying desperately to come up with a halfway credible answer. Ashamed, he managed to croak out a weak, "no, I haven't."

Brenda: "Why should you? Livin' in your clean, little white world. (Then granting him a bit of leniency) Mr. Maaaaann, you sure do have a heap of learnin' ahead of you."

Dick: (sheepishly): "Yes, indeed I do."

Driving into a blazing sun that Friday afternoon, Dick tried to buoy himself up by concentrating his thoughts on his arrival at Hardee's in Marianna, where he always celebrated his weekend beginning with a big cheeseburger, fries and Diet-Coke. Today, try as he might, he couldn't shake off the events of the past week, this seemingly endless series of up and downdrafts, rattling his psyche to the core. Every time he thought he had gained a modicum of *Oberwasser*, finally having gained the upper hand, he found himself once more forced into facing his abysmal ignorance, his book- learning knowledge suddenly of little use, in fact, in many ways an additional burden. Fact was, that appellation applied to him twelve years ago, when he was pruning trees in the orange groves on those stultifying long days in the groves, and although he hated admitting it, still possessed a certain validity, even today. *College boy*, that was the moniker given to him by his older co-workers, who saw him as a temporary intruder from another, foreign world, a stranger in their midst. Here too, he was basically considered an *outsider*, despite all efforts to obtain some form of recognition that, he too, belonged to the ACI community. For the white staff members, he was a strange amalgam of ultra-liberal European culture attached to a Don Quixote attitude regarding his eagerness to "awake the curiosity" of the inmates, to "bring out the best in them" – come hell or high water. As for the blacks, having become Panhandle veterans, they cooly awaited to see if this young, inexperienced academic could really *walk his talk.*

Following the riot last May, the administration had gradually begun to implement new programs aimed at preventing similar outbreaks of violence. Bible classes were revved up and a new, young woman counselor had been hired, who immediately introduced, much to surprise (and skepticism) of the older custodians, a course in meditation for those inmates willing to make an attempt to "tune in, drop out" of their harried everyday life at ACI, slowly learning to relax, control their emotions. The chief counselor, Mr. Duncan, whom Dick, much to the merriment of the inmates, had given the moniker *Dunk'n Donuts*, also had his doubts, but was willing to begin a test run.

It was around this time too, that Dick gained further insight into an area overlooked during his first months at ACI. Basically there were two types of Title II teachers at the institution. Those like Dick (and his predecessor), Joe, and a few others, who merely saw ACI as a temporary stepping-stone in their respective careers, definitely not planning a long-term stay on the Chattahoochee. As for the others, and this dealt practically only with those teaching over on the high side, there seemed to be that one goal all were striving for - but one never, ever mentioned in conversations. Namely, that much envied and long sought job was that of being a counselor, which meant no longer stuck in a classroom with 25-30 recalcitrant inmates, teaching ten different classes per week; for the counselors had their own office, where they faced the inmates in an almost intimate atmosphere, on a one-to-one basis, no longer having to deal with a class full of young, restless men. No, here the tables had been turned, here the counselors had the upper hand, held the high cards, with the inmates mostly doing their level best to put on a good face, show a bit of remorse, humbly explain their needs. This often occurred in a almost sheepish manner, sometimes even poignant, the inmates hoping not only to have some immediate needs taken care of, but also well aware that a positive, co-operative attitude just might effect their EOS, now having become the dominant date in their lives. Dick took no umbrage at this thought, the goal of counseling, knowing full well that he too, in a similar situation, would be a Johnny-on- the-spot when it came to applying for such a position. Still, now he viewed the relationships between the various teachers through a slightly different perspective, sensing the hidden competition between them.

That weekend saw him going to bed after having watched a rather mediocre late movie on Cannel 13, Panama City. Awakened from a deep slumber by the telephone in the living room, which continued to ring incessantly, he was forced to heave himself out of bed, staggering into the living room to answer the phone. Glancing down at his wristwatch, he noted that it was 3:30 am, thinking who in the hell could be calling the house at this ungodly hour? Surprised, even startled to hear his brother's voice on the phone, he concentrated, trying his best to shake off his fogginess of mind.. In a calm tone, his brother explained that on his trip back from Panama City he had briefly fallen asleep, whereby the car had left in road in the middle of a slight curve, over-turning and crashing into some dense shrubbery some fifty yards from the road. Having been buckled up, Jim had survived the wreck in good stead, excepting a sore shoulder and missing his glasses which had flown off during the crash. Dick was then given rather specific direc-tions as to where the accident had taken place out on highway 231, with Jim asking him to please drive down to pick him up. Pleased that his brother had gotten off so lightly with no major injuries, Dick agreed, telling his brother that he'd be underway in ten minutes, proba-bly arriving in approximately a half hour.

Jim's directions had been relatively concise, considering lack of easily identifiable landmarks in the area of the rather flat, pine-studded coun-tryside, with Dick driving the last five miles or so with his high-beams on, finally spotting his brother on the left side of the road, flagging him down. Drawing closer, he also saw the car, seemingly almost undam-aged, way off the road in some palmettos. Once out of the car and talk-ing with Jim, it seemed as if the car had left the road at 60 – 70 mph, then hitting a small dell, had either flipped end-over-end or spun around on its axis. At any rate it had landed on all four wheels before finally coming to a stop. Jim, more concerned about his missing glasses than the car, asked Dick to help him search the vicinity around the car's path, saying he had already checked out the car's interior. Dick figured that the car must have spun on its axis through the air after hitting the dell, hurling Jim's glasses out the window, so he first started checking the dew-tinged grass along the car's flight path, aided by the dawn of a clear Florida day. After five minutes of scouring the area, Dick indeed came upon the glasses, intact, unbroken. Later, back home in Marianna, Jim ate a quick breakfast before diving into bed, having said that he'd learned his lesson about drinking too much and driving too late, with Dick wondering how much the repairing of the car would entail, nevertheless considering his brother of having a guardian angel for having survived literally unscathed.

Wouldn't you know it, Garcia wasn't due to be in class until Thursday since this was his long week over at the construction site, thus postponing again the chance to meet with him privately. It was during this waiting period that Dick once again mulled over the risk of passing on a book to an inmate. Morally he hadn't the least qualms; legally, however, he asked himself if this were proper, not wanting to break prison rules, be they written or unwritten. On the other hand, he felt it was his duty, not wanting to renege on his promise, also feeling that the feats of Cesar Chevez would be a positive influence on those hispanic inmates reading the book, ergo he didn't waver.

Since the cleaning crew always arrived some ten minutes late after the class had been released at two o' clock, Dick had told Garcia in advance to see him after class, Garcia's shiner had healed in the meantime, with hardly a trace left. It really gave Dick a thrill to see Garcia fondle the paperback, eager to dig into the text. His eyes shining, the young man thanked his teacher for the gift, allowing Dick the chance to pose a few questions:

Dick: "Tell me Garcia, what's a nice guy like you doing in a place like this?"

Garcia smiled, catching the gentle reproach, also realizing that his teacher seemed genuinely interested in his case.

Garcia: "I was young, inexperienced and got caught up in a group of people in the hispanic community down in Miami running an illegal bolito operation, you know, illegal betting. Basically that's what got me two years."

Dick: "Better than having been sentenced for armed robbery, right?"

Garcia: "You're right about that. But lemme tell you, there are some really bad dudes in here, some crazy guys. But hey, I'm not afraid 'cause I got friends, know what I mean?"

Dick: "Yeah, I've been told if one of you hispanics are attacked, the attacker has to deal with the whole latino group, who come running to their buddies' aid."

Garcia: "Yep, we're tight, you have to be. There's some real mean people in here, so you have to keep your back covered at all times."

Dick: "As for the book, well, you don't remember who gave it to you, right?"

Garcia (with a little laugh): "Nope, no idea. Can't seem to remember."

That weekend saw Dick and Joe DeChristoforo drive over to Tally to catch the new Monty Python film "The Holy Grail". Dick had already seen it some weeks ago, but Joe implored him to go again. What amazed Dick was the fact that the jokes came so thick and fast that, with the second viewing, he found himself laughing at lines he had simply missed the first time around. The two were also together in Marianna, watching the sixth game of the World Series when Carlton Fisk blasted his historic home run, around midnight, his body language urging the ball to stay inside the foul pole. Seeing that his uncle Hap had been a big Red Sox fan and that the team had their winter quarters down in Winter Haven, well, no wonder that Dick supported the Sox.

A glance at his calendar sufficed to tell him that if he were going to congratulate Fredi and Bärbel on their upcoming wedding, well, the weekend would be his last chance before the event took place. So, realizing that there was a time-difference of seven hours, he decided to give them a call Saturday afternoon around 1:00 pm CST. Digging through a long list of addresses and phone numbers he finally came across theirs in Berlin, amazed that he still had it. Upon dialing the number, he hoped that they would be home, it being a Saturday evening in West Berlin. Tensely he listened to the largo tempo of the beep...beep...beep, thinking perhaps they were indeed out on the town.

Then, with a slight click, the phone was lifted and a soft, gentle, warm shower of words, phrases delighted his senses, leading him back to the *Studentendorf in Schlachtensee*, where he had met her for the first time. Their first date entailed a long bus ride to the *Philharmonie*, with her entrancing him through her ability to not only understand his broken German, but also because she possessed an ability to *really* converse, not dominating nor timid, just winningly *normal*. He was so taken with her – and bitter when she was taken away from him – by the man she was just about to marry. Even now, not having seen her since well over three years, she spoke much as if they had merely not seen each other since a couple of months ago. Amazing! Soon, all to soon, he heard his voice in the background demanding "Who's on the phone", and her reluctantly passing it on to him, resulting in an immediate change of atmosphere, the warmth giving way to a much cooler, reserved and clipped tone, evoking the feeling that the interest in the call was minimal. Consequently, the whole conversation lasted about five minutes before Dick was able to blurt out a belated congratulation to the wedding und Fredi thanking him, adding that maybe they'd see Dick once more if he were ever to visit West Berlin again, then, with a click, the phone call was over. Sitting down with a sigh, Dick moaned that this meant that the extremely slight chance that anything could ever come of this tiny hope was now forever dashed. Another woman gone to the dogs. That was all he needed, such a call, he being alone with little chance of any female companionship now or in the near future. "*Hätte, hätte, Fahrradkette*," he thought grimly. Better yet, "*Klappe zu, Affe tot.*"

A Day in the Life

Returning from work on November 18th, he sat down and commenced putting down on paper the events of that late afternoon, when he and Lawton drove back from ACI to Mariann, both of them engaging in typical conversation concerning the situation at the institute, the two not only letting off steam, but also clearly staking out their own positions vis-à-vis the daily problems of teaching in a prison. Weaving through a mixture of pick-ups and "Detroit iron," the baby-blue Kharmann Ghia slipped past poultry and headed into a bright late fall sun on highway 92 west. The following conversation ensued:

"Goddammit to hell, I lost my gloves today!", blurted Lawton.

"Who took 'em, inmates?", queried Dick.

"Yeah, I shoulda known better than to bring 'em. These bastards will steal anything not nailed down. (Slight pause). I wished to hell you could use blasting caps, you know, blow their goddamn hands off. They'd steal your shit if you shit on the floor! Bunch of goddamn idiots!"

"You know Eddie Wolfe?"

"Yeah."

"Well, I ended up giving him a *speeding ticket* today, although, actually, he's a damn good student, but he was supposed to be filling out a work sheet I had passed out."

"And?", Lawton ask eagerly.

"So I caught him scribbling around on some paper, hadn't done a damn thing. That's why I gave him the *ticket*. Later, when he came back from the office, he told me that it was his first ever at ACI. Now that'll keep him on his toes for the near future. Don't you think?"

"Fuck the inmates."

"You're getting too bitter Lawton."

"No, I'm not bitter, it's just that I'm sick of trying to teach a bunch of goddamn ignorant fuckers. Today, for example, I was tryin' to explain to some bastard how he was costing the state of Florida some $10,000 a year just to keep him in prison. When I broke down the costs, you know, custody, food, electricity, he protested, sayin' 'whut you mean electricity? It don't take no electricity to keep me here.' That dumb son-of-a-bitch!"

"We're now up to 1027...should be close to 1200 by Christmas."

"They don't give a damn, just pile 'em in here. You know we're gonna go to close- custody."

"Bullshit."

"Wait and see."

The Kharmann Ghina slid into the left lane to avoid those crawling pick-ups turning right, heading home.

"What are you doing over Thanksgiving", asks Lawton.

"I'm dropping down to Winter Haven to see the family and some friends."

"Too bad, I was gonna invite you over for some Thanksgiving puddin'."

"Why don't you ask DeChristoforo?"

"Na."

Long pause ensues.

"Hey Lawton, you heard who's comin' back to the US? Eldridge Cleaver."

"Yeah, I heard."

"Seems as if he's seen the light. No more of this black against white. You know, it's like he's finally grasped that economic, class differences are paramount."

"Dammit Mann, you're crazy as hell. Lemme tell you something – there's always gonna be racism and that's a *fact of life*. You just got a bunch of lazy fucking niggers on welfare who are retarded and lazy as shit."

"Yeah, but you got to understand the social conditions, their backgrounds."

"Shit! Oughta castrate the fuckers. Cut their nuts off when they're two years old!"

"I say educate 'em, give 'em jobs!"

"Jobs my ass. They don't wanna work, lazy bastards!"

"Goddamn Lawton, what you expect? They government keeps them on welfare instead of creating jobs - think of Roosevelt. In the ghettos they've got over 40% unemployment. Inmates tell me they *want* to work, but can't find a job... thus they end up turning to crime."

"That's pure bullshit, Mann. Now listen, I got a lotta friends who didn't finish high school and are *rich today*. Shit, they pulled themselves up by their own bootstraps, instead of havin' a lot of fucking babies."

"Sure, that's one of those guys you knew in Panama City, having his roofers nail down roofs with *ten-penny nails*, ripping off the buyers and..."

"Jesus, Mann, stop giving all this liberal crap! I say sterilize the bastards!"

"Why are you so goddamn bitter?"

"No, no. I just hate working for an organization like this one where people without college degrees are calling the shots. Look at Willwright, doesn't even have a degree of any kind – just a GED. And what about Collins? He got his job through influence, friends, pull, the right connections, that's all it is."

"So, it's not who you know, it's who you blow, right? No, all kidding aside, tell me something Lawton – what's a guy like *you* doing in a place like *this*? I mean with you having an *M.A.*?!"

"Well, I fucked up. They wouldn't give me a job after my B.A. – said I was *too draftable*, so I ended up going back to school. Now, get this;

after I received my M.A:, I was told I had *too much education*! In fact some little prick over at the state employment office had the balls to tell me 'we don't have jobs for people with M.A.'s.' The little fairy face only came up with one offer: *sewage disposal in Miami*! Six years of college for *that*?!"

While listening intently, the driver nonetheless kept a sharp lookout for cops on the four-lane stretch to Grand Ridge.

"Well, you shouldn't have gotten a degree in public administration. My God, what the hell did you choose to get a degree in that area?"

"Hell, I was just looking for a job."

"*Any* job?"

"Hey, this was way back in the late sixties when the job market was quite open, so I figured that public administration was a good shot. Now *everybody* wants to go to college and get a high-paying job. What a crock. You know what they oughta do? Dammit they should limit enrollments."

"In other words, you got *your* college degree, now the other poor devils should be prevented from having the same chance you had, right?"

"Damned right!"

"Now that you're on the bandwagon, no one else is allowed on, correct?"

"Lemme put it to you straight. There are simply *too many* people going to college who don't wanna work when they come out. They're all lookin' for a desk-job which pays big bucks. For example, take Duncan. Hell, he doesn't do shit. A real suck-ass. That's how he got his promotion."

"Lawton you poor soul. You'll still be here next year, pissing and moaning."

"No I won't. I've got several applications in right now: UCI, Cross City, Lantana – just you wait and see. I'm not gonna put up with this shit for another year. No way!"

Long pause.

"I'm going over to Tallahassee after work on Friday, so don't wait for me."

"You drivin' Monday?"

"Yeah."

"It's O.K. with me as long as you make it up on Monday."

"Shit, I'm not *that* cheap."

Hitting the blinker, the driver pulled into the big Winn-Dixie parking lot.

"Damn Mann, what's that noise? It's coming from up front."

"I think the tire is too big, too much air. It's rubbing against a device that the former owner had installed when he had the air-conditioning put it."

"Nah, that's not it. It's the break-shoe if you ask me. It's shot."

"You're crazy, it's the tire."

"Bullshit. Just you wait and see."

"Don't lose any sleep over it. See ya tomorrow at seven sharp."

Before getting out of the car, Lawton turns toward Dick.

"I'm headin' home to get some groceries – man can my wife *cook*! Hey Mann, when you gonna get yourself a little lady, huh?"

"Who knows? Don't think it'll be soon though."

"Well, you better step on it, or you're gonna be too late. All the women around here done all been caught. Know what I mean?"

"I'm not fishing in *this* pond."

Lawton, now out of the car and sauntering off.

"You'd best be gettin' on the stick or you'll be runnin' out of stock."

Early Thanksgiving morning the "Gang of Four" (Dave, Jim, Dick, Doug) headed south, driving south from Tally all the way down to Winter Haven in central Florida, a long haul. Dan and Betty were driving up from Miami. As a kid, using a Phillips 66 road map and a ruler, Dick had figured that from Pensacola down to Key West, one would be driving around 850 miles. Wow! Of course, Florida wasn't Texas, not even Alaska, nevertheless such a distance in one state was quite something. Since they had started out so early in the morning, they soon felt the pangs of hunger, deciding on the spot to stop in Perry for breakfast, choosing a little restaurant on the outskirts of the town.

In a boisterous mood, the four young men entered the half-filled restaurant, finding a table by the window much to their liking because it was round in form and giving each person just enough elbow room. Had they been a bit older or perhaps a little wiser, they would have surely noticed the other customers giving them the eye, not accustomed to such a loud, early morning invasion of four guys who were certainly not from the local area. Although not particularly dressed up, their clothes were definitely not commensurate with small town tastes. To make matters worse, they talked up a storm, with a seemingly jovial disregard of the languid atmosphere preceding them. Jokes were flying thick and fast when the large, over-weight waitress finally sidled up to their table, flipping down four menus, and curtly stating that she'd be back when they were ready to order. They being ravenous, it didn't take long before all four were ready to order, awaiting the waitress to return. If they had been more aware, more perceptive, they would have had a better grasp of their growing predicament, instead killed time by feeding off each other, in a ring of constant, hearty conversation. Gradually, they began to glance around, eagerly awaiting the waitress to return. Finally, Dave managed to spot her, giving her the high sign that they were ready to order, something she merely acknowledged by a brief nod, signifying that she'd be there in her own sweet time to take their orders. Some five minutes later she appeared, a sourpuss expression plastered across her face, gruffly noting the dishes wished, then stalking off to the kitchen, leaving four puzzled faces behind, all wondering what had caused this disrespectful service. This incident did nothing to impair the festivities, with Doug egging Dick on to show Dave the routine from the Broadway musical "Top Banana", where a guy walks up to a friend saying, "I just came back from the fruit market with three bananas and I'm going to give you one of them..." ending with the punch line, "you eat the *third* banana!" All these monkeyshines undoubtedly didn't go unnoticed within the restaurant that sleepy Thursday morning. When the orders arrived 15 minutes later, they were placed on the table, with the waitress promptly turning on her heels and walking away. Later, after the bill had been paid, Dick suggested each of them place a penny on the table beside each plate, showing that they too could make perfectly clear their distaste of the manner in which they had been treated. Once back in the cars, they discussed the incident, in which, through a closer analysis, it became obviously unmistakable that they had been seen as what they were – a bunch of young men with college educations, slightly raucous perhaps, maybe even giving the impression of being a little condescending, something they had simply overlooked at the time, not having their cultural antennas *auf Empfang.*

Thanksgiving also meant cramming the five Mann boys back into their old bedrooms of yore, not a difficult task since they had also become used to close quarters through their years in the Navy. The turkey was delicious as well as the rest of the meal, topped off by making a short, color film plus a photo of the five out in the front yard, all lining up in front of Jim's dull-orange Opel, all young, healthy and happy. However, one thing in particular had changed, rather drastically. In the sixties, Thanksgiving had always meant using those three days, Thursday, Friday and Saturday, to receive old high school friends at 144 or visit them at their parent's home for a warm, friendly get-together, a chance to revive old friendships and keep abreast of what others were up to – jobs, military service, marriages, etc. Those days were now long gone, with most of the fledglings having left the nest for other cities, states, even foreign countries. Of course, the parents were still glad to welcome the unexpected visitor, but they too had aged, many retired or standing just before it. When thinking it over, yeah, ten years was a long time.

All through those days at home, Dick did his best to avoid any one-on-one conversations with his parents, fully aware of what that would entail, namely a whole litany of questions to which he felt himself backed to the wall, simply unable to answer. Now that Dave, Doug and Dan were married, as with most parents, his too were ever hopeful that there would soon be grandchildren on the way, or at least planned for. Here he would be batting .000, not even having a girlfriend. Cleverly managing to circumvent any such one-on-one situation, he, nevertheless found himself suddenly alone with his father because Dave and Jim were out at the Parks family at Lake Cannon, while Doug was driving his Mom out to visit some friends, leaving Dick and his Dad alone in the living room watching a college football game. At half-time his father abruptly turned off the TV, engaging his son in the following conversation:

Dad: "I can tell you one thing – we're glad to see you all five back in the corral again. It's been a long time you know."

Dick: "Yeah, we're glad to be back. As you always say – 'Don't break up the five."

Dad (curious): "Well, what I'd like to know is this. What are your future plans, just what do you have in mind? I mean, damn, you're thirty-three years old. Dave, Dan, Doug are married, have jobs, and here you are working in a prison, you with all your college degrees!"

Slowly but surely Dick could feel his temper start to flare because this was just the probing questions from his father which he wished to avoid. What fired him up more than anything else was the fact that *he himself* was so unsure as to his future plans, thus this unwanted intrusion made him just that more nervous and aggressive.

Dick: "Dad this is just a *temporary* job, merely another step down the path. O.K.?"

Dad: "A path to where?"

Dick: "Well, er, that would mean graduate school. Now do you see?"

Dad: "And where would this be? Gainesville? And when?"

Dick: "It all depends on so many different factors, especially the financial angle. Ever since the Veterans Administration told me I couldn't use the last eight months of my GI Bill for graduate school, well, I've been stymied."

Dad: "Stymied my ass. Why don't you find a *real* job that corresponds to your qualifications, hell, you've been studying for how many years now… ten, eleven, *twelve*. Twelve years! It's time you turned all that knowledge into *bucks*. Don't fiddlefart around anymore."

The absolutely worst thing about his father's criticism was - that it was *true*! He had been stolidly ploughing ahead in his academic career in a more or less steady course until the conflict with the VA. Now that had really thrown him off track. As for the present, well, he was just treading water and that's exactly what his father sensed, thus the *quo vadis* question.

Dick (almost timidly): "Well, I've been keeping up on my Chinese, in fact, even considering returning to Taiwan in the late spring to improve my abilities before deciding on which graduate school to apply for."

Knowing that this nebulous reply might suffice to stop his father's onslaught he hoped that they could now change topics, talk about something else. Ignoring all the flim-flam Dick had used to bring this interrogation to an end, his father continued to bulldoze straight ahead.

Dad (adamantly): "Damn your time, you're still just fiddlefarting around, *no* decent job, *no* girlfriend, God knows where you'll end up. Of the five brothers, you're the *odd-ball*. It's time to get your ass in gear – *grow up!*"

With these scathing remarks ringing in his ears, Dick slunk out of the living room like a beaten dog. Years before, he had been the one to lash back at his father, counter all his arguments with a blistering verbal repartee, and now he was the one slinking away, unable to muster a convincing reply to the onerous criticism piled upon him. Indeed, there was nothing else to do but hunker down, take the shots as they came and hope that, this too, would pass. As bitter and angry he was at his father's caustic remarks, he took solace in the knowledge that his Dad carried a heavy burden too, working at the shipyard in Tampa, driving up to 100 miles a day back and forth, and all this with him now pushing 65. Nevertheless, Dick knew, despite all his efforts, he'd always end up at the bottom of his father's totem pole. That's just the way it was.

That evening over diner a slight dissonant tone crept into the otherwise jovial chat at the kitchen table, when the brothers got into a ruckus concerning their jobs. Dave and Dan started teeing off on Jim and Doug for having "soft" positions with the national and state governments respectively, stressing the fact that working in the "market economy" meant *really* having to work hard, face tough competition, all the time in the realization that their job was *not* secure (as Dan was soon to find out). Of course, Jim and Doug took umbrage at this, stating that they too suffered from low pay, tough bosses and the general inefficiency of bureaucracy. But the mood never degenerated into a serious spat, so consequently, the verbal blows were basically of a powder-puff nature with no one losing their cool. Dick, observing this with a modicum of distance, was glad to be out of the spotlight, after the unpleasant event in the afternoon, pleased to get the monkey off his back.

Dark December

Nine long years ago had seen Dick in his senior year at the University of Florida sharing an apartment with Jerry Pfeiffer, receiving his first GI Bill checks, taking a course in German history and becoming friends with a law student living in the same complex. Dino K., who originally hailed from Tallahassee, but, nevertheless turned out to be a real Gator fan, cottoned to Dick right away when discovering that Dick too, was a Catholic plus a true orange and blue Gator fan. Both used to often spend a half an hour tossing the ball around in the late afternoon, talking sports, politics and women. When occasionally visiting Dino, Dick marveled at the reams of yellow legal paper his friend had written for his law school courses, impressed with Dino's industriousness. Dino also proved to be a real mover and shaker in campus politics, pulling strings behind the scenes, seeing to it that *his* fraternity's candidates were elected into positions of power on campus. If one were looking for grit combined with savvy, well, Dino K. had a plethora of both.

Although being the state capital, Tallahassee never claimed to be a metropolitan area of any renown, its real importance lying in housing the legislature plus the large public administration as well as two big universities. It was in this world of small-town intimacy that Jim had perchance found himself in a brief conversation with a certain Dino K., mentioning that his brother had studied in Gainesville too. Naturally, it was merely a matter of seconds until Dino found out that he was talking to Dick's brother, both astonished at this unexpected relationship. Dino gave Jim his telephone number telling him to make sure Dick called him up the next day. Sure enough, the following evening Dick called up Dino, surprised at the warmth at the other end of the line, giving Dick the impression that only a few years had gone by, with Dino eager to meet his old buddy from Gatorland again.

During his drive over to Dino's house, he mulled over some information about his friend which Jim had managed to obtain from various sources. It seems as if Dino, after finishing law school in Gainesville, had returned to his native Tallahassee to establish a law practice. Evidently his well-oiled connections on and off campus had paid dividends, since he was soon taken in as a partner in a locally well-known law firm. In the seventies he had made a name for himself by defending the former Superintendent of Education, who had been charged with corruption, although he lost the case, with the defendant spending several months in a federal prison, but Dino's reputation actually rose, him being seen as an honest lawyer who did his level best to protect his client. When he arrived at the house, which turned out to be more of a small, southern mansion, Dick asked himself how one could have managed to accumulate so much money within the relatively short period of six years' time.

Dino's warm welcome made Dick immediately feel at home, bringing back fond memories of his senior year in Gainesville, which, of course Dino raved about, but not before introducing him to his comely wife, who, quickly split the scene leaving the two men alone. A curious person by nature, Dino wanted to know just what his friend had been up to since they last saw each other in the summer of 1967. Gladly Dick attempted to compress those eight years, particularly those in Berlin and on Taiwan, not forgetting to add the sob story ending, about being turned down by the VA and thus having to work temporarily at ACI. Listening with evident empathy, Dino posed several questions as to his general opinion of the cultural differences between Germany, China and the US, with Dick trying to give a halfway balanced answer, admitting freely that each culture had its own values and beliefs, stressing that one could always learn something valuable from other countries, some things being rather easily transferable, others either with difficulty or, perhaps not at all. Walking over to the fireplace, Dino showed Dick photos of his two cute young daughters, praising, like any proud father, their manifold achievements in school. When asked if he planned on having children, Dick winced slightly, before mumbling an empty phrase intimating he just hadn't found the right girl yet. Taking the hint, Dino dropped the subject, inviting his guest to come up to his study on the first floor for a cold beer and a chance to listen to a radio broadcast of the Florida-Miami game being played down in the Orange Bowl.

The game turned out to be close, much closer than they had originally thought likely. Throughout the game, Dino, rumbled on about Florida's striking inability to win an SEC championship – an elusive butterfly, a will-o'-the-wisp always just a few wins away, but never attainable no matter which teams or which coaches. Both men sang praises of Gator Ray, the Florida coach who presented fans with their *first* Heisman trophy winner: Steve Spurrier! Dick too had been a student in those four years when the young man from Tennessee rose to stardom, with the former basking in the warm glow radiated by the quarterback's success. Wasn't that great? Dino, swiftly squashed Dick's ebullience. Hey, that was great, way back then, but where was the follow up - the SEC title, national recognition as a top ten team? Seeing that the game down in Miami was far from over, with the Gators merely leading by four points, the two friends became increasingly nervous, tied to the radio broadcast like an electronic umbilical cord, twitching, yowling with every play. Then, in the middle of the fourth quarter, Miami was forced to punt. The Florida player, however, failing to judge correctly the ball's trajectory *fumbled the ball*! Luckily it was recovered by one of his own teammates. Nevertheless, this set off a spasm of loud cursing by Dino, who double-damned the player for dropping the pigskin at a moment like this. Dick tried his best to mollify Dino's outburst, explaining that the young man was just a *freshman*! My God, merely a first-year, second stringer, with little real-game experience. It took all of Dick's efforts plus another cold beer before Dino cooled down some, with Dick now trying to change the subject by proffering questions regarding his host's wife and kids. After the game ended with a 15-11 Florida win, they closed shop for the night, Dick promising to keep in touch and thanking Dino for the invitation that evening.

On the drive back to Doug's house Dick had plenty of time to reflect on that which he'd just seen. Both of them having been born in 1942 meant that, in a way, they had the same chances, time-wise. They were both relatively hard workers, also pretty intelligent. So, how was it that Dino already had a very well-paying job, a beautiful wife, two children plus a big house, whereas Dick had pitifully little to show for all his academic success? Lord, whatever did Dino think to himself about Dick's present low- trajectory career? After all Dick's talk as a student in Gainesville about later working for the state department in Washington, that all seemed just hot air today. The only grimm joke that came to mind was that at least he was working *at* a prison, not spending time incarcerated *in* one.

By the beginning of his twelve month of teaching, he had long begun to sort the inmates into various and sundry categories ranging from inveterate trouble-makers to those with whom he gradually cultivated a type of loose friendship – for the age difference between them often only amounted to less than 12 years. While some were strongly extroverted, others kept mostly to themselves, speaking when spoken to, quiet and calm, rather introverted individuals. The bulk of the inmates, however, fell into that broad range of "normal", indicating that one could communicate with them readily, when necessary. Thomas Evans, 20 years old, a curly-head young man of Dick's own size and weight, sat on the far left side of the second row in the class starting after lunch, at 1:00 pm. Arduously studying for his upcoming GED, Thomas, never one to initiate a conversation, had come up to the desk to have his teacher explain the meaning of some scientific term, when, in leaving, he mentioned not feeling very well. Asking for more details Dick discovered that his student had a "heart problem" since early childhood. which was a probable explanation for him feeling ill. At any rate, when class was over Dick called over to Thomas "to take it easy" as the inmates filed out. About an hour later, underway from the front office to his classroom he thought he heard a siren in the distance, a sound which only lasted for some seconds before being silenced, with Dick not feeling the least perturbed, having long become accustomed to all sorts of strange events transpiring at the institute.

When taking roll the next day for the first class after lunch he noticed that Thomas Evans was absent, a bit unusual, but nothing completely out of the norm. Perchance, as the bell rang finishing the class, Dick spoke to one of the inmates leaving:

Dick: "Hey Dowdy, come over here for a second. I gotta question for ya."

Dowdy: "Yeah, what's up? Whatcha wanna know?"

Dick: "I noticed that Thomas Evans was absent today. Know if he's on a special work detail, or maybe sick?"

The inmate blanced noticeably, giving Dick an incredulous glance.

Dowdy (hesitantly): "I, I thought you got the word, I thought you knew."

Dick: "Knew *what*?"

Dowdy (slowly): "He's *dead.*"

Dick (shocked): "Dead? When, where, how did it happen?"

Dowdy: "Well, at Phys. Ed. we were all supposed to run a lap, you know, to warm up. Thomas wasn't feeling so hot, so he told the teacher he'd rather not run."

Dick: "And did he run?"

Dowdy: "Yeah, the teacher chewed his ass out, telling him he'd better run if he knew what was good for him. So Thomas took off running."

Dick: "... and then?"

Dowdy: "Well, about half way through the lap Thomas just collapsed, you know, just fell down, stopped moving. I think the teacher thought at first it was a joke, that Thomas was pulling his leg. Musta been a minute or so before people really started to worry, realizing something musta gone wrong."

Dick: "Dammit, what did the teacher do?"

Dowdy: "He sent for the doctor, who, when he came, tried his best to revive Thomas, who lay there unconscious."

Dick (groaning): "Oh my God, the poor kid's lying out on the field, not receiving proper treatment. Oh shit, what did they do then?!"

Dowdy: "Well, they placed a call over to the general hospital in Chatta-hoochee and told them to send an ambulance, pronto. But when it ar-rived, well, hell, he'd done been dead for some thirty minutes."

Dick: "You think he coulda been saved?"

Dowdy (thoughtfully): "Yeah, maybe. If he'd been treated immediately, you know, on- the-spot. But thirty minutes, nah, that's just too long."

Thanking the inmate for passing on the information, Dick awaited the arrival of the cleaning crew, looking forward to gaining their input re-garding this tragic event, further disappointed in discovering not only their barely peripheral knowledge of the fellow-inmate's death, but also their lack of empathy, much the same as if some bothersome fly had been swatted away. The group seemed to see this as a *natural* situation, unfair, detestable to be sure, but not anything to get too upset about in a completely overcrowded prison with each inmate trying to take care of himself – well, and maybe a few, carefully chosen buddies.

Over a spaghetti supper that same evening, brother Jim commiserated with him in regard to having lost two students in the past six months, also underlining the terrible fact that both were merely twenty years old. Attempting to cheer Dick up a bit, Jim mentioned that Doug had called earlier inviting the two of them to take a short canoe trip down the Chipola River this coming weekend, wanting to show Dick the tricky and "dangerous" water falls aptly called look & tremble. Nodding in half-hearted agreement, Dick dejectedly walked into his bedroom to read the latest edition of *Die Zeit,* hoping to digress for a while from those morons thoughts spinning around in his mind. Try as he may, he couldn't focus on the article he started reading, his brain unable to wrap around the theme, caroming off 180° in another direction, ratch-eting the time-frame back to last March when he had first heard the news of Bob Howard's rampage out in Louisiana, an insane outburst which had not only taken his own life, but also that of two other completely innocent persons. A month later, Steve Hollie, murdered in less than one hour, after sitting quietly in Dick's classroom. And now this, a young man, who, despite his pleas of not feeling well (with his heart condition), forced to run a long lap. Then, after collapsing, was first castigated before the teacher finally became aware of the true situation. That plus the long, excruciating wait for the ambulance from Chattahoochee to arrive, only to find that all aid was now in vain. Adding insult to injury, he thought of the recent meeting with Dino in Tallahassee, with both being the same age. Seven years had past since their bonding that year in Gainesville, both parting ways in the summer of 1967. Dino had acquired a law degree (summa cum laude), joined a successful law firm, married, brought a house and fathered two daughters. And Dick? To his B.A. he had added a *Diplom*, only to find himself working in a prison, instead of teaching at a university. A true all-around loser, with nobody to blame but himself – that was the *worst* part.

Flowing out from the region south of Dothan, the Chipola River runs through Jackson county on its way to a confluence with the much larger Apalachicola River, which later empties into the Gulf. In fact, it also runs through Mariana and on down past Altha, where Doug's wife came from. In those past years, Doug had done a lot of kayaking there, also diving for Indian arrow-heads, even managing to discover a few lying in the river. That Saturday, with the temperatures being in the mid-sixties, saw Jim, Dick and Doug launching Jim's canoe effortlessly into the Chipola River, gliding down towards Altha. Doug, in a boisterous mood, had brought along three cigars to commemorate the day, which he noted, which was rather unusual, since seldom would the Mann kids be a threesome, not to mention all four or even five being together – excepting holidays, of course. Thus Doug was of the opinion that this should be promptly celebrated, ergo the cigars. Dick, a stolid non-smoker, could be seduced into puffing on a good stogey on a propitious occasion – like today. Not having to paddle much because of the steady current, all three enjoyed the moment, smoking their cigars on that sunny afternoon.

Soon they perceived the sound of rushing water ahead of them, signaling that they were approaching the series of rapids given the name of Look and Tremble by the local natives. Whereby, in all honesty, these were merely a category 1 falls, perhaps at the most, a 2. However, being indeed the "only show in town" on this rather placid river, the locals had created the name with tongue-in-cheek, also wanting to draw interested visitors too. So the Manns arrived at the rapids with Dick in the bow, Jim in back (with all his white-water experience), Doug resting in the middle between the thwarts. However, upon their arrival, Doug suddenly stood up, bracing himself with his calves against the gunnels, despite Jim's admonishments to sit down. Some ten seconds later it happened. Suddenly, the canoe plunged downwards and to the right, throwing Doug off balance, forcing him to grab hold of a gunnel to his left, which, in turn, almost tipped the canoe over, allowing water to pour in over the side, while Jim and Dick desperately tried to stabilize the canoe. Nevertheless, even if they were successful in not capsizing, they were now forced to head for shore, their canoe, half swamped, lying low in the water. Upon reaching land, Doug leaped deftly out of the canoe, leaving it up to the others to empty the craft of water. Standing in water up to their chests, Jim and Dick held the stern and bow firmly in their hands. With Doug cheering them on from the sidelines, they managed, with a great effort, to turn the canoe on its side, allowing the bulk of the water to flow out, before they heaved it into the air to empty the rest. Afterwards, they attempted to lunge out of the water back into the canoe. But wait, what's this! When Dick tried a scissors kick to propel him up into the canoe, he found his legs almost numb.

Holy hypothermia! The cold water had robbed his legs of all energy, forcing him to exert maximum efforts with his arms, in order to slide, step-by-step over the gunnel and back into the canoe. In the past, he had indeed, heard the term hyperthermia, but never *experienced* it! As planned, Doug stayed in Altha while Jim and Dick drove back to Mariana swearing at the frivolousness of their younger brother and with a little more respect for Look & Tremble than they had had before.

Loping over to the Print & Supply Office during his afternoon break, seeking an extra allotment of a certain textbook, Dick found himself in an innocuous conversation with Mr. Henderson, the young, black office head, when, unexpectedly the front door opened, and in breezed Clarence, big as day. Turning toward the inmate, Dick inquired as to his well-being:

Dick: "Hey Clarence, how's it going?"

Clarence (nonchalantly): "Same as usual. I like working here in the office."

Henderson: "Yeah, he's been a big help to me. Quick on the up-take, if you know what I mean. A quick learner, know what I mean?"

Dick: "Yep, he's a fast one alright."

Clarence: "Mr. Henderson told me that you studied over in Germany, correct?"

Dick: "Yeah, spent some five years over there."

Clarence: "How did you feel, I mean living along with former Nazis?"

Dick: "Well, things have changed since WW II. West Germany is a democratic country now. Why does that interest you?"

Clarence: "I'll tell you why. My father taught me that Nazi Germany and the US certainly had several things in common."

Dick: "For example?"

Clarence: "Take those racial laws passed in Germany and compare them with those Jim Crow laws in the southern states. Now, does that ring a bell?"

Henderson: "Ha, he gotcha there Mr. Mann!"

Dick (stunned a bit): "Er, well, you're right in way. It all depends on..."

Clarence (interrupting): "You're simply blotting out reality. My father came back from WW II and found out that not one damned thing had changed. Now what the hell was he fighting Hitler for? It doesn't make any sense – the struggle is *here*, at *home*, in the *states!*"

Henderson (tauntingly): "Well, Mr. Mann, what do you have to say about that?"

Dick (hesitantly): "O.K., I admit that he has a point there. Brenda also informed me about the Claude Neal case and..."

Henderson (stopping him): "Hell no, man! He's talking about something else, about Cellos Harrison. Ever heard of him? He was lynched here in Jackson County during WW II. Back in 1943, to be exact. Hell, just over thirty years ago! Now tell me sumthin' – how do you expect us to be fightin' for the US, when you're lynching black men left and right. Bet you never heard of that case either, right?"

Dick (stumbles): "Er, no, I wasn't aware of all this. No one had ever mentioned it to me, just never knew, never realized ..."

Dead silence in the room.

Dick: "Well, I'd better be getting back to my classroom now."

Clarence (triumphantly): "Yeah, go back to your classroom, where you're the boss, with no one challenging you and your white science. Man, you still got a long way to go."

Dick left the office in a blue funk. My God, was he ever pissed off! Clarence had nailed him to a cross, showed him the true lay of the land, embarrassing him in front of Mr. Henderson. Of course, the real reason behind Dick's anger lay squarely in his own inability, no, his unwilling-ness, to add 2 + 2, simply connect the dots, something which he had deliberately avoided since high school. Sure, back then, he'd sensed a vague similarity between Nazi Germany and the daily segregation of southern life he'd grown up with, having become used to it, even com-fortable, even if he'd occasionally utter a slight word of criticism with his family or group of friends. Damn, here he was at 33, just starting to grasp the whole dimension of the problem.

A week later, Dick drove over to Tallahassee to catch a flic, spending the night at Doug's, with the latter entertaining his older brother with some fine scotch whiskey and a relaxed conversation in front of a blaz-ing fireplace, with Doug openly admitting that such a fire wasn't actual-ly necessary, but that he enjoyed the atmosphere which it gave the room, a fact which had Dick nodding his head in agreement. Shifting from politics to his personal development, Doug emphasized his growing disenchantment with his job, underlining, as he had before, the tediousness resulting from a seditious micromanagement; i.e., on the one hand the staff was given great leeway in doing research on improvements in the area of retirement, however, on the other hand the order of the day, chiseled in granite, called for all colleagues not to "make any waves", a stern, rigid commandment for all employees. Consequently, Doug had been sniffing around, looking for a *real* job, where he could better employ his talents - perhaps also earning a higher salary to boot. At present, being low-man-on-the-totem-pole, Dick heartily agreed, repeating a quote from the famous New York lawyer, Louis Nizer, that "nothing is work, unless you'd rather be doing something else".

Over breakfast the next morning, Dick innocuously broached the question as to when Doug and Karen planned to show up down in Winter Haven for Christmas, adding that he and Jim were planning to drive down late on December 23rd, so as to be there in plenty of time for Christmas Eve. Without batting an eye, Doug replied that they weren't sure exactly when they would leave Tally, thinking they'd probably follow suit, arriving roughly around the same time. No sooner had these words been uttered, then there was a loud shout from the neighboring room, "Doug, come in here for minute, I want to talk to you!" The tone of voice sounded more like an order or command than an invitation, perhaps an unpleasant harbinger of things to come. Five minutes later Doug appeared back at the breakfast table with a *whole, new* idea. This change of plan now entailed them driving down on the 21st instead of the 23rd. Immediately, Dick asked him why so early, when the other brothers wouldn't be arriving until the 23rd, with Dan and Dave coming in perhaps early on the 24th. It simply didn't make any sense. Still, Doug stuck to his guns, stating they would be leaving on the 21st , and that was final! Wanting to avoid the situation from getting out of hand, Dick suggesting that he would talk with Jim about this. Maybe Doug and Karen could see their way free to coming down on the 22nd instead of the 21st. Driving back to Mariana he wondered what his older brother would say to this fresh news.

When told of Doug's plan, Jim said he smelled rat. Rat? Why was his brother so suspicious? Was Dick somehow not in the know? There, sitting on the living room couch, Jim explained to his brother many unknown facts, which began way back in the year Doug and Karen had married in 1972. That year, being gracious, Doug spent Christmas at her parent's home. The next year, just before Christmas, Karen fell ill, unable to make long ride down to Winter Haven – as planned. In 1974 Karen spent the holidays with her parents, according to the schedule adopted by the newly married couple; even years in Altha, odd years in Winter Haven – everything even Steven. Jim concluded that Karen was actually reneging on the spirit of the agreement since it seemed as if they planned to leave Christmas Day in order to be back up in Altha for a big noon meal there. If this be so, then that means that Doug and Karen are giving us the double-shuffle, morally breaking the accord made, promising an equal deal for both families. Just like Dick, Jim wanted to wait a while, talk to Doug privately when they were down at 144, an argument to which Dick quickly agreed, seeing that Christmas was right around the corner.

Two days before Christmas Eve all was quiet at ACI, Dick scenting a slightly morose feeling among the inmates, much as if their minds were wandering homewards, towards parents, wives, kids, relatives and friends. Showing a dab of empathy with these lonesome young men, he decided, for one day, to drop the normal class schedule and instead, have the inmates put their thoughts on paper – in whatever form they wished to choose - a story, a poem, a sketch, whatever suited them. The result astonished him. No sooner had he told the class his plan, than the inmates, almost jumping the gun, began writing, heads down, fully

180

concentrated on the empty sheets of paper handed out. At the end of the day, he had collected some 95 papers, some relatively short, others pages long. That evening at home he sat at his desk perusing them, pleased that most of his students had taken the task seriously and done their best to express their intimate hopes, fears, desires in various forms and according to their backgrounds, some well-scripted, others merely scribbled, a few showing a brief flicker of insight, the rest a ragged compendium of random thoughts, seemingly jotted down on the spur of the moment, leaving a handful of inmates with exceedingly well-expressed thoughtfulness, joined with powerful emotions. Casting his eyes down on the stack Dick grinned, *tja, so isses*. On one hand so much mediocrity, nevertheless, despite all odds, a few gems were to be filtered out – as the quote went, *E pluribus unum*. Although most of the written work tended toward a run-of-the-mill category, a few stood out from the others due to their originality, sharp insights or straight-talk, detailing the inequities of prison life interspersed with saddened *mea culpas* for the rats tail of problems they had lumbered upon their wives, kids, parents, friends; and endless litany of self-pity mixed with flashes of true contrition. One inmate waxed eloquently about waking up in his *black* bed, taking a shower in his *black* bathroom, having breakfast in his *black kitchen,* then putting on his black clothes, departing his black house only to be blinded by a *white* day! Then there was another one of his inmates, a small, unassuming, bespectacled young black teenager named Willie, who had the appearance of a 9th or 10th grader. Glancing down at his paper, Dick had some difficulties deciphering the jumble of words all written in a fine, almost feathery style slightly reminiscent of an art deco design. However, the contents proved to be cryptic in nature, with the teacher unable to make rhyme or reason out of the text. Leaning back in his chair, Dick sighed, this kid was in desperate need of psychological aid, and here he was locked up in prison!

The long ride down to Winter Haven from Tallahassee, broken briefly with a quick stop at *Frog's* for some good pork barbecue sandwiches, saw both Jim and Dick deftly avoiding delving too deeply into the gathering crisis regarding Doug's lack of full-time presence during the short family get-together at Christmas, both of them awaiting the arrival of Dave and Dan to add pressure on Doug to finally *see the light* and at least spend Christmas Day at 144. Thus a whole panoply of themes were discussed, ranging from their jobs at the social security office or at ACI. Along with this, football, high school days, the Navy, and assorted friends were all subjects to which both brothers, no slouches when it came to talking up a storm, easily whiled away the time, with Jim graciously agreeing to drive down highway 33 so as to enter Winter Haven via Lake Alfred.

Arriving at 144, they found that Doug and Karen were out visiting one of Doug's old high school buddies, with their Mom and Dad sitting glumly in the living room watching television, greeting their sons cordially, but not with the usual verve and vigor they expected, the reason for this being that Doug had already dropped the bomb, telling his parents that he and his wife would be leaving sometime around noon ,or shortly beforehand, on Christmas Day, meaning that the family would merely be together for some 24 hours seeing that Dave and Dan would be arriving around noon the next day. Dick told his Mom not to worry, he and Jim would talk to Doug when he returned, convinced that the two of them could pressure their brother into staying at least for another day so that the *whole* family could enjoy Christmas Day together. This was something they owed to their parents! Unfortunately for them, Doug and Karen returned late in the evening, giving the two brothers no opportunity to corner their brother for a heart-to-heart talk.

Since Jim thought it wiser to wait until the reenforcement arrived, Dick used the morning to visit the Soderlundts, who were interested to see what the fifth son was doing teaching in a prison up in the Panhandle after having spent so much time studying overseas. Although both parents were quite careful not to be *too* candid, it was obvious that they were somewhat disappointed in the abrupt downward spiral of Dick's academic progress. Mae couldn't come to grips with him having visited them last year, hot to trot to begin his Ph.D. courses at Florida State, only to discover to her chagrin that, instead, he deigned to teach in a prison way out in western Florida, in the *boondocks* so to speak. Heroically, he availed to explain the strange interpretation of the GI Bill offered by the Tallahassee veteran's office forbidding the use of funds for post-graduate studies, with the Soderlundts shaking their heads in simultaneous disbelief. In an effort to avoid any questions regarding his future plans, he questioned them as to what their own sons were doing and, further fleshing out this theme, went off on a long, drawn out tangent as to just what his brothers were involved in, dodging, of course, the present problem at 144. After mumbling a few last words about seeing them again at Easter, he drove home, thankful to have left the miasma behind him, that odious stench of once again having gravely disappointed those who had had such great expectations.

By the time he returned to 144, Dave and Dan had already arrived, quickly deciding on a course of action with Dave, of course, taking lead, later to be followed by Jim and Dick working in tandem, with Dan standing by to lend a hand if necessary. As was his usual wont, Dave, seizing an appropriate moment, shunted Doug aside bluntly accusing him of ruining the Xmas holidays by reneging on the agreement made years ago, according to which Doug would alternate his Christmas visits, one year Altha, one year Winter Haven. Doug couldn't have his cake and eat it too. Dave's chastisement was interrupted by their Mom announcing that it was lunch time for the family, providing Doug with a providential break. Nevertheless, less than an hour had passed when Jim and Dick asked Doug to accompany them on a walk around the neighborhood, with the latter reluctantly agreeing. Walking together down 1st Street, then vectoring over to Avenue C, Jim and Dick, using the *good* cop, bad cop method, berated their brother incessantly; with the former pleading with his brother to consider for a moment his *parent's* feelings in the matter, particularly their *mother*, who placed great worth on a festive dinner on Christmas Day. Not missing a beat, Dick then proceeded to rain a barrage of verbal blows upon his brother regarding the *double-shuffle* of the past years, demanding that Doug fulfill his part of the bargain *completely* and not waffle, cease the equivocating! Meanwhile, while his brothers continuously ratcheted up the pressure, Doug marched stolidly along, as mum as King Tut, only occasionally uttering a soft "No, I see it differently" or "That's what *you* say". By and large, he took the verbal punches without flinching, although his brothers could tell that their arguments were having an effect. Just before arriving back home, Doug managed to obtain a brief cessation of hostilities when he added, "Well, I just can't decide this by myself, I'll have a discussion with Karen and then we'll decide." And thus the showdown was postponed until later.

Midnight mass at St. Joseph's saw the church chock-a-block with worshipers, all scrunched into the pews facing a brightly lit altar announcing a high mass in store. Having arrived some thirty minutes early in order to get good seats, Dick used the time to scan the pews, looking for familiar faces. Just the same as last year, he had great difficulty in ferreting out the contenance of old friends of the family from the 1950's or even high school friends, since, well, fifteen years had passed, and not only had the number of friends diminished, but a whole raft of new ones had suddenly appeared. For Florida had now become a boom-state, whose population had tripled since 1950, meaning that the newcomers were swiftly outnumbering the *oldtimers*, the native-born *crackers* of his youth. He even saw a small number of black people – something unthinkable back in the segregated 40's and 50's. Adding to his misgivings was the knowledge that the bulk of his high school friends had long left the town and, like he himself, had no plans on ever moving back. While his Mom buried herself in her missal, Dick reminisced of those days of yore when he was an altar boy at the old St. Joseph's church, where, partially hidden behind an angel bearing a tall, white candle, he could observe the rows of parishioners assembled, of course, always checking out those cute young Catholic girls sitting beside their parents. It was a God-like feeling, this being able to see others, but not being easily visible oneself. But those days were long gone, along with those oft mumbled Latin phrases – *ad deum qui laetificat, juventutem meam christe/kyrie eleison, et cum spiritu tuo* finishing with a firm *dominus vobiscum*. Now, being up-to-date, masses were held in English. However, when the long line for Holy Communion began forming, emptying the pews around him, he definitely felt even more of a renegade, a turncoat, at any rate an outsider, sitting alone by himself, disdained by those who knew him. It being already past 1:00 am when the mass had ended, his Mom showed little interest in chatting up other women, so that they soon arrived back home, both incredibly hungry.

Dave and his wife Marilyn had decided to skip mass and help out cooking up a humongous late-night breakfast with all the trimmings - pancakes, scrambled eggs, toast, cereal, orange juice, cold milk, the works! Afterward, there was the requisite offer of wine, whiskey or Dr. Pepper, serving to relax some of the interfamily tension of the past day. Everything seemed to be going along smoothly until Jim and Dick, in the midst of some chit-chat concerning the upcoming pig-roast in Mariana, saw their Mom approaching them, her faced pale, her mouth tightened. They were told in a low tone, that Doug had just passed on the word to her that he and Karen would be leaving around 4:00 am in order to return to Altha. Completely stunned by this, Jim and Dick saw all their cajoling, pleading having come to nil, with their younger brother obviously placing Karen's family before his own. Damn traitor! Now there was nothing else to do than accept this sudden *fait accompli* and deal with it, as hard as it may be. Just then a phrase popped into his mind, one that he remembered from his days on Taiwan - 吃 苦 *chi ku* – eat bitterness. That's exactly what he felt now, his holiday spirits blown out like a candle in one short puff. With the nimbus of Doug's sudden departure hanging over their heads, the Christmas Day dinner transpired in a rather awkward fashion, with all present trying their best to clearly overlook the smudge on the family honor, attempting to be somewhat *too* jovial, *too* carefree. Glancing over at his Mom, Dick thought he could ascertain that she was laughing on the outside, crying on the inside. A real bummer.

Upon driving back to Tally the next day, both Jim and Dick made a conscious effort not to rehash the events of the past few days considering the issue moot since the injuries had been inflicted with little sign of remorse from the other side, no tidings of seeking to recompense for damages rendered, ergo it was better to stop crying over spilt milk, what had been done was done. *Finito, Schluß!*

Years later, when reviewing the events more calmly at a greater distance, Dick realized what a asinine mistake he and his brothers had made acting like a bunch of goddamned fools! Unbelievable that Dave, who had studied psychology for a while at Florida State, with Jim having taken some courses too, couldn't have grasped how counter-productive their actions had been. Dick too had had a year of psychology with Mrs. Whitney at WHHS, where he'd been an avid student. Nevertheless, they had all committed the grievous error, which was hard to forgive; namely, that of having placed their brother in a situation where they were forcing him to choose between them and his wife. What fools they were, demanding that he place them before his very own spouse! How could they have been so blind, didn't they possess a single ounce of empathy? Hadn't they been told manifold times that one's first allegiance was to one's wedded wife? Willfully, they had obtained just the opposite of that which they had hoped for – much like in Newton's Third Law: For every action there is an equal but opposite reaction. Here was Dave with his intimate knowledge of physics! A lot of good it had done him.

Entirely New Perspectives

The winter months in Florida, exactly the time of year where he remembered his Mom blossoming like a flower, exuding a joy which radiated throughout the family on those cold, frosty mornings in January, particularly when her husband, always up by 5:00 am at the latest, had already had a fire blazing in the living room, in the fireplace in the middle of the stone wall at the far end of the room. For the kids, the downside was having their mother force them to wear coats to ward off the cold, only to have them lugging the coats home that afternoon in the warm, bright sunshine. Those halcyon days of dry, cool air with a cloudless, deep blue heaven, where occasionally B-47s from McDill Air Force base would spin fine, gossamer threads of silver-white condensation high above central Florida, were treasured by the whole family. Late Sunday afternoons, returning from pick-up football games down at Denison Field, often meant joyously discovering that his Mom had made lots of hot tomato soup along with grilled cheese sandwiches, all washed down the glasses of cold milk. Winter season also meant sleeping longer and deeper, in the crisp air, no longer bedeviled by the humid heat or intruding mosquitoes. For the same reason, nearly all the camping trips with the scouts took place from October to April. No wonder the *snow birds* started heading south in the late fall – knowing the innate quality of a sunny, cool, dry Florida winter.

Subsequently, the once tense atmosphere of those sultry summer days at ACI had long vanished, giving way to a more placid climate both in the dorms as well as the classrooms. In fact, Dick nodded in amazement when Mr. Sexton, meeting his teacher in the hallway, cordially wished him a Happy New Year, adding that he was awfully pleased to see what Dick had accomplished in the last year – not one of his inmates had to be sent to lock-up and, moreover, the number of his students passing the GED test had shown a noticeable increase. Inordinately pleased to receive this praise, Dick knew this meant less pressure from above, something which now seemed to be a thing of the past. His relations to the other teachers were, with one or two exceptions, positive because the new ones respected his teaching skills and rapport with the inmates; the older ones friendly, since he was open about himself not planning to make a career out of teaching at ACI, and thus was no longer considered as a possible competitor for one of the few office jobs available to Classroom II teachers. Consequently, he now began to use this social capital in order to enlarge the radius of his contacts within and without the educational compound.

At the beginning he had found himself, as could be expected, hovering on the edge of the "lunch bunch", that heterogeneous group of teachers and staff members which coagulated regularly around noon in the prison cafeteria, waiting to be served their lunch by those inmates working the kitchen. While there was no set seating order, there was an unwritten rule that good friends would sit with another; those not possessing such a close relationship would then form a loose circle around them, much like electrons revolving around the protons. Being new and of an unknown quality, Dick quickly found himself shunted out on the group's periphery, him seen as an "outsider", not yet ready for full inclusion. Of course, as the months passed by he gradually, in a process of slow osmosis, began to gravitate more and more toward the core of this social galaxy, now and then arriving too late, he found himself again in an outer orbit. Nevertheless, by the fall of that year he had managed, thanks to the subtle aid of Brenda, to gain admittance to tables of the older employees, the glowing center of this spiral nebula.

This being 1975 and in the cracker panhandle, one would have expected, and indeed found, a certain self-chosen segregation in regard to seating arrangements. Nonetheless, this was *not* the Florida of the 40's and 50's with a rigid separation in schools, hospitals, bus stations, etc., but a post-civil rights era, in which black teachers and staff members were slowly but surely becoming commonplace, not always warmly welcomed, but accepted, tolerated. In the cafeteria, which actually resembled more of a lunch hall, this separation between black and white still held true, as a rule, but there were exceptions. The dining area where the teachers and staff members met was such a spot, where there was an overlap, a mixing, with no fixed places to be sure, since everyone arrived in waves, at slightly differing times, which led to gradual, tentative amalgamation of those sitting at the lunch tables. As one would expect, many of the staff members (and some of the teachers) were locals, hailing from such small nests as Dellwood, Rosedale, Cypress, Sink Creek or even Sneads itself, the town abutting the institute. In these circles, Dick was seen as an anomaly, a square peg in a round hole, an over-educated intellectual, damned by some inexplicable fate to end up teaching in Jackson county. Indeed, all this also lent him the advantage of making himself a certain center of interest among several staff members, them being curious to know more about this *Sonderling* who had suddenly appeared in their midst.

One bright, crisp day in January found the theme of conversation at the "center of the galaxy" revolving around the relatively new television program *The Jeffersons*, which concerned the economic rise of a black family from Queens to New York's upper East Side. The program was a spin-off from *All in the Family*, which, week for week, listed the ordeals of a certain Archie Bunker, a white, middle class American who had trouble adapting to the swiftly changing social environment of the 60's and 70's. George Jefferson, a black man and one of Bunker's former neighbors, having had great success in business, moved on up to the East Side with his wife Louise and son Lionel , encountering new problems he thought he had left behind. Situated at a table beside Brenda and sitting across from one of the black girls from the front office named Louise, Dick mentioned that he too had seen some the latest episodes of *The Jeffersons* and found them quite amusing, a statement which was received in wide-eyed bewonderment by Louise.

Louise (quizzically): "You mean to tell me you been watchin' *that* program?"

Dick: "Sure. It's funny, and, not only that, but a bit critical to boot. Don't ya think so?"

Louise: "Yeah, it's funny, but now you *know* there aren't that many black folks livin' up there on the East Side, right?"

Brenda: "She's gotcha there Mr. Mann. That's just a TV program, made by white people."

Dick: "Well, yes, it's basically written mostly by whites, but it *does* reflect, to a certain degree, the way some blacks think and act. Or am I way off base?"

Louise (laughing): "Oh, you white people. Always lookin' an laughin' at us. Just like that Archie Bunker. But he's just sayin' what he thinks. Now I know…"

Dick (butting in): "You can't conflate all this. You can't speak about *white* people as if all of them think or live the same way."

Brenda: "So, you're sayin' *you're different.*"

Dick (defensively): "I can tell you one thing, Joe DeChristoforo and I think a lot differently than most of the other white guys working here. That's for sure."

Louise: "Hold on, I think I hear the preacher man a comin.'"

Realizing that the conversation was quickly taking a turn for the worse, Dick decided on a little verbal jiu-jitsu.

Dick (with a heavy accent): "Yo damn right Weezy, I done come to save your young asses!"

A second of silence ensued. Then Brenda broke out laughing, with that loud, deep, hearty sound he knew so well.

Brenda: "Mr. Maaannnnn! Now what has gotten into you? How come you talkin' like that? You better cool it."

Louise (quizzically): "What's with this *Weezy*? You tryin' to be like George Jefferson?"

Dick: "No way, honey. Jest tryin' to show ya that you shouldn't try to lump all *white* people together. Get it? Jest can't say that all *white* people be de same. Now, am I right, or am I right?"

Brenda; "Mr. Mann, why you puttin' us on?"

Louise: "He jest be makin' fun. Playin' the clown."

Dick: "Jest tellin' you how it *is*."

Brenda and Louise (almost in chorus): "An we know how it is. Amen!"

The very next day he received a short letter from Li Shi asking him if he was serious about returning once more to Taiwan, strongly implying that her patience was thinning, practically demanding that Dick come to a final decision in the matter. Still unable to fish or cut bait, he, as so often, temporized, replying evasively to her latest missive by writing a long letter, basically filled with empty phrases, cumulating in the statement that he would *soon* let her know *for sure* when he would be returning. Eager to end on an upbeat note, he dug out his small book on Chinese poetry from the Tang dynasty, sending her a cryptic message from Li Bai (李白):

状 前 明 月 光, 疑 是 地 上 霜

举 头 望 明 月, 低 头 思 故 乡

The English translation reads:

Before the bed moonlight came. I thought it to be frost.

Looking upward I gazed at the moon, bowing my head with thought of home.

Alone the word 乡 gave his heart a twinge because it signified *Heimat* in German, and, should the character 愁, be added on, it would then mean a yearning for the *Heimat*; plus realizing that, at the age of 33, he now had at least a full one-third of his life behind him, with little hope in the immediate future of finding a wife and having children. Moreover, as they say down South, he wasn't sure of just *where he belonged to be*. Should he still try for a Ph.D.? Or should he return to Taiwan? Or, perhaps he should simply return to Germany, seeking a job there? At any rate, such a decision would have to be made in the coming weeks, so he'd have to steel himself and soon cross that looming Rubicon, despite all fears and doubts.

In late November, Joe DeChristoforo had mentioned something about some guy asking for volunteers to play on a city league basketball team he was setting up in Marianna. Dick, moderately interested, told Joe that he'd like to join the team once everything had been officially organized. Sure enough, two weeks later Joe reported that practice was to begin next week, with the first games scheduled for mid-January. Ronnie W., a young, local businessman had paid the $50 dollar registration fee, asking Joe if he'd help coach the team, getting it into shape for the coming season, to which Joe readily agreed.

What football was to Dick, basketball was to Joe. Having captained his school's B-squad basketball team in Orlando, he possessed all the skills of a good player, able to dribble, pass, shoot and defend. He also was a born play-maker, able to swiftly analyze an opponents' weakness and quickly set up offensive plays to exploit it. His enthusiasm, however, was dampened by the fact that, although 12 players were registered, only eight or nine would show up for practice, either having to work a shift, being sick, or just a general lack of interest. Realizing that no one on the team had ever gone beyond pick-up games, Joe did his utmost in trying to instill a certain pattern of play when on offense, with him, as a guard, using hand-signals to announce the start of a specific play. Despite his well-meaning intentions, the other team members thought this a bit too complex, too confining, spoiling their quest for fun, for spontaneity, somehow limiting their own individual talents. This reminded Dick all too well of the flag football team he had played with back in Gainesville in the fall of 1966; a team which, having such experienced players, refused to practice, figuring their talents alone would ensure them victory. Alas, they continually lost to inferior, but more well-organized teams. Now, here in Marianna, Dick couldn't shake the creepy feeling that, once again, the team, in failing to pay heed to Joe's experience, would end up playing below their worth.

It was about this time that the new Bob Dylan album *Desire* appeared on the market with a song that gave Dick an electric jolt. Not having been an especially great Dylan fan, he had never purchased an album, merely satisfied to listen to those songs he would occasionally catch on the radio. However, this new album contained a song Dick felt had been especially written for him: *Hurricane*. For exactly this song seemed to congeal all the anger and frustration pent up in the last year of work at ACI, a damning indictment of the racially biased system of justice in the US, based on the trial of the boxer Rubin Carter, where the police are obviously trying to frame an innocent man. The words slugged the listener with verbal body shots:

Rubin Carter was falsely tried
The crime was murder "one", guess who testified?
Bello and Bradley and they both baldly lied
And the newspapers, they went along for the ride
How can the life of such a man
Be in the palm of some fool's hand?
To see him obviously framed
Couldn't help but make me feel ashamed to live in a land
where justice is a game

Admittedly, Dick had to smile wryly over the fact that his own situation was miles apart from what Dylan was singing about, not just geographically, but with his inmates being solely so-called *first offenders*, ergo, why get so upset over these young hoodlums, punks, rift-raff, who deserved spending time for their offenses. Some twelve months ago, such a mindset roughly corresponded to his attitude when he arrived at ACI. And in the meantime, he had heard an endless litany of complaints, some of which were obvious confabulations, chockfull of contradictions, with the inmate being the *innocent* victim, not the perpetrator! Nonetheless, there were cases, however, in which Dick found the sentences handed out simply too hard, too disproportional for the crime committed. He distinctly remembered one hayseed from out in the Panhandle, who had received three years in prison just for the possession of *two* reefers in his pocket! Of course, that was just the tip of the iceberg so to speak, since his black inmates told similar, but even more heinous stories regarding the institutional racism inherent in the judicial system, which always concluded with putting the onus on minorities.

As usual, the word came in via the unofficial channels of the ACI grapevine, which never failed to offer some choice tidbits regarding particular events dealing with inmates. That very afternoon, members of the clean-up crew had jokingly spoke of an altercation the other day during Bible class. It seemed that one of the black inmates, supposedly under the influence of Clarence, the Black muslim, had accused the Jews in general, and Israel in particular, of being capitalist blood-suckers, exploiting black people, and that the cancerous growth named Israel should be annihilated. To everyone's great surprise, however, the teacher, Mr. Toupee, sternly took the wayward inmate to task, singing praises of the establishment of a Jewish state after WW II, very supportive of those Jews returning from abroad, to once more set roots in their native land. While the work crew rattled on gaily about other, unrelated themes, Dick did his level best to wrap his mind around the info just received. Now, what was this? What could account for this outbreak of *philosemitism* in this back-water, Bible belt institution? Was that which he had just heard really the truth? Whatever, he was now determined to get the word straight from the horses's mouth, so to speak, by setting up a situation in which he could personally suss out Mr. Toupee's opinion over this thorny subject.

196

Sure enough, two days later, during the lunch break, Mr. Toupee dropped by the classroom to deliver a bulletin, allowing Dick to engage him in the following conversation:

Dick: "Excuse me, but I just read recently where some preacher maintained that God allowed the Holocaust to occur in order to bring the Jews back to the land of Israel. Do you think that's true?"

Mr. Toupee: "Yes, basically, that's true."

Dick: "So, you support the return of Jews to the Holy Land, right?"

Mr. Toupee (now lighting up): "Shoot a mile yes. Whole boatloads of them!"

Dick (astounded): "Whole *boatloads*?!"

This he hadn't expected. A southern Baptist deacon calling for the return of Jews to the Holy Land, that over-heated caldron, where the so-called Yom Kippur War had taken place just a few years ago. Think as he might, he couldn't make any sense out of this.

Dick (with a touch of desperation): "But why?"

Mr. Toupee (surprised): "Don't you see? That what the Bible foretells, don't you know? Read the Holy Scriptures, Daniel, Ezekiel, that's their prophecy! Haven't you ever read the Bible?!"

Wham! With one powerful stroke, the ball was back on his court, with him bereft of any means of returning the shot. Not particularly *Bible-fest*, he felt himself clearly in defensive position, unable to deal with the art of the exegesis now facing him.

Dick (stumbling): "Er, not really. I mean..."

Mr. Toupee (brusquely interrupting): "Well, have I got news for you. Read Matthew 24: 32-33, for example. It's clear: The gathering of the Jews in Israel is a prerequisite for the Second Coming, a fulfillment of the Biblical prophecy, which portends the apocalypse or the end times."

Dick (truly astonished): "How did you come about discovering all this?"

Mr. Toupee (triumphantly): "Let me tell you how. By simply reading the best-seller The Late, Great Planet Earth by Hal Lindsey, who relied solely on the Holy Scriptures themselves as a solid foundation for his book. It's all in the book, the threat of war in the Middle East, an increase in natural catastrophes such as plagues and famines, the revival of Satanism and witchcraft, all clear signs of that the Second Coming is nearer than we think."

Literally saved by the bell which rang for classes to begin, Dick once again remembered what a local inhabitant had said regarding those people living in Jackson county. Either they were working for the state, farming, or they were preachers – perhaps, sometimes too, a little bit of all three.

What had begun in such an innocuous manner as to hardly have caused a blip on the radar screens, barely a tremor on the political seismographs, sudden sprang into national headlines, providing an unexpected theme for lunch-time conversations – and beyond. The reason lay merely some 100 miles north of ACI, as the crow flies, in Plains, Georgia, where, in late 1974, Jimmy Carter had announced his candidacy for President of the United States, causing a wave of amazement. Unimaginable, the chuzpah of this mediocre, one-term governor of a deeply southern state, believing himself to be a viable candidate nationwide. "Jimmy who?", ran the headlines of many newspapers, while Carter quickly slipped off the scope, his quest seen as quixotic at best, hardly mentioned afterward by the national press, radio or TV. Consequently, the surprise was absolute when Jimmy Carter gained the most votes of any Democratic candidate at the Iowa caucus! Topping that, in February he won the New Hampshire primary too! In literally no time at all, Carter's presidential bid had become the talk-of-the-town; and this went for ACI too, where many staff members were enthralled by this totally unforeseen development. Lunch-time saw Dick witness the following conversation:

Mr. Lawton: "No doubt about it – the man is making history. Who woulda believed it, a candidate from the Deep South, now that's a first!"

Ellen Sue: "Yeah, but what about LBJ?"

Mr. Toupee: "No, honey, he was from Texas, way out west! Not from Dixie!"

Mr. Lawton: "That's right, he's a *southern* boy. Hot damn!"

By now the spark had flown over to a neighboring table.

Mr. Blanton: "And you know what? He's a peanut farmer, following a family tradition, so he knows the lay of the land. Why he'd be a boon to us out here in Jackson county."

Mr. Lawton: "Not only that, the man was a naval officer, graduated from Annapolis. Even studied nuclear science and…"

Mr. Mann (breaking in): "...which makes him a *nucky-poo.*"

Mr. Lawton: "A what?!"

Mr. Mann: "A nuclear engineer. We had a whole raft of them on the Enterprise."

Using a slight pause in the conversation, Mr. Toupee now let the cat out of the bag, having waited for just this moment.

Mr. Toupee: "You're all forgetting the most important fact, one which will have an enormous impact on the whole United States."

Mr. Lawton: "What's that?"

Mr. Toupee (proudly): "Jimmy Carter is a professing *born-again* Christian! A deacon in his local Baptist church, where he teaches Sunday school."

Now completely electrified by the turn of events, Ellen Sue begins a swift chautauqua regarding the importance of Christian education at home and school, stressing the 10 commandments as a guideline for a healthy society.

Ellen Sue (aglow): "Here's the man who'll take the Bible off the bookshelf and put it back into our lives, just as he's made Jesus Christ the *first* priority in *his* life. I heard that he said that 'he'd never tell a lie or make a misleading statement.' I think that *all* Christians should support his candidacy!"

Mr. Toupee: "Amen, sister."

Now, in the cooler winter months, Dick found he had more time to work with individual inmates since the classes had been successfully *domesticated*, with only an occasional disciplinary problem. While some were relatively open to his approaches, others remained closed, ensconced in their own private world, despite all efforts to gain their trust and cooperation. Such a case was Tommy Weathers, a 17- year old, who was doing time for manslaughter after shooting and killing another young man with a revolver. With his wavy brown hair, his cherubic face, not yet fattened by age, he never let on to being the slightest bit remorseful regarding the shooting itself, steadfastly maintaining that "it had just happened", the whole incident being seen as "an event beyond his control". In some inexplicable manner, it almost appeared that he was even perversely proud of his deed, leaving Dick unsure as to a possible reason for this strange attitude, surmising that, perhaps, Tommy was using this as a defense against other inmates, warning them not to provoke him. Nevertheless, Dick realized the need for psychological treatment, all the time clearly aware that the chances of him receiving the same were practically nil. Once, in a longer conversation with the young man, Dick had, treading softly, casually mentioned the possibility of some kind of aid or therapy, anxiously awaiting Tommy's reply. The question only served to evince a sly smile from the inmate, who simply refused to consider the matter further. Now and then, sitting behind his desk up in front of the classroom, Dick would observe Tommy staring into some distant world, with a hang-dog look of some one completely lost, reminding him of those lines sung by Johnny Cash in the *Folsom Prison Blues*:

When I was just a baby,
My mother told me son,
always be a good boy,
don't ever play with guns,
but I shot a man in Reno,

just to watch him die,
now that train just keeps a rollin',
I hang my head and cry.

Dammit, there he went again, dribbling the ball leisurely up-court, nonchalantly, moving his endomorphic ass so slowly, deliberately, as if he were in a game of horses, not in a city league basketball game. Nonetheless, it was Ronnie who had forked over the 50 bucks registration fee, making it *his* team, with *him* the captain; God, did that ever piss Dick off since there was nothing else to do but grit his teeth and wait for the first pass to really start the action. This subdued anger soon led to an unwise move on his part after some five minutes of play. Seeing that his team was failing to get enough offensive rebounds, Dick, a mere 5' 9", decided to mix it up in the paint, going high in the air for a ball off the basket, only to be blasted out of the way by one of the more powerful opposing players. Coming down awkwardly, he immediately felt the sharp pain, having pulled a muscle in his lower thigh, thus thobbling off the court to let a substitute replace him. Luckily for Dick, the pulled muscle healed rather rapidly, allowing him to begin playing again some two weeks later.

In retrospect, he often thought of the song *Wunder gibt es immer wieder,* a tune he had heard back in Berlin in the early 70's, since what he experienced on that cool, clear, sunny afternoon out on the concrete walkway between the buildings was, in every sense of the word, a small wonder. Sitting at his desk, correcting test papers, he looked up to see a group of inmates and Ellen Sue; conversing out in front of the classroom, obviously engaged in a serious talk. Curious, he went out on the plaza, intent on finding out what was going on. Approaching the little group, he was a bit surprised to see Zeke Daniels speaking with Ellen Sue; Zeke, who had been loath to talk at all, despite all of Dick's inquisitive attempts. A bit shorter than Dick, with stubby, blond hair and pale face, he had proven to be a quiet, rather mediocre student, mostly keeping to himself, while, at the same time, indicating to other inmates that he was not a man to be crossed. Some thirty seconds after Dick arrived, Zeke turned to him, thanking him for all the effort he had made on the inmate's behalf, telling his teacher that he regretted not having taken his class studies more seriously, vowing whole-heartedly to do so in the future. Stunned by this, Dick managed to burble out a reply, which, basically, posed the question as to what event had led to this change of attitude on Zeke's part? Before the inmate had a chance to open his mouth, Ellen Sue jumped in, stating that this *conversion* was due to the Bible study course, which had certainly led to Zeke's finally *seeing the light, changing his tune*, now ready to lead a truly Christian life. Not willing to take her argument prima facie, Dick turned to Zeke, asking him if he himself was able to give a rational explanation for this this sudden transformation from Saul to Paul. Squinting into the slanting rays of the sun, the inmate calmly replied that he had done a powerful lot of thinking in the last few days, then coming to the conclusion that *he*, not his parents, teachers, police, was at fault. It was *he*, who had misused the trust of others, neglected his duties and lost the respect of his friends and family. When further pressed to name the root cause for this revelation, Zeke smiled, merely stating that he had come to this conclusion on his own, after a great deal of contemplation, adding, perhaps as a sop to Ellen Sue, that the Bible study course surely hadn't hurt him either. Later, driving home on highway 90 into the dull red orb of the sun, Dick now mulled over the events of the afternoon. How to best explain this ungodly complete role-reversal he had just witnessed? Was this really an epiphany, a manifestation, wherein Zeke had attained a flash of insight as to the causes of his present situation? Had those Bible study classes actually provided stepping stones for the inmate's psychological house cleaning? Whatever, one thing was sure – this was a positive development and Dick was determined to follow Zeke carefully in the coming weeks to determine if this metamorphose was of a lasting nature. Still, whatever the reasons were, this buoyed him up immensely, a sign that there *was* light at the end of the tunnel.

His injury now healed, Dick eagerly awaited the next basketball game, which Ronnie announced at the next practice session, and which finally saw the team ready to learn the basic rudiments of play-calling per hand signals. After practice, Ronnie told them that he had a little *surprise* in store, for the next game would be against a city league team from Panama City! It seemed as if one of the local teams, due to injuries and sickness, had to call off the next match, with the team from Panama City graciously agreeing to make the long drive up to Marianna in order to fill the open date. With no further information available, they all assumed that this was just a normal, city league team.

No, you didn't have to be a basketball coach in order to quickly size up the players arriving early that evening from Panama City; all big, all white, all having played high school basketball together. Not a good sign. Before the game commenced, Ronnie told his team that one of the opposing team members couldn't make the drive up, so they'd only be playing against *four* players – four against their five! A piece of cake! Dick wondered where Ronnie's brain was; had he failed to take a good look at the other team? My God, the shortest guy was six feet, the others around six two or six three. Observing their warm-up's, Dick recognized immediately that his team would be facing a well-oiled machine, running on all cylinders. And so it came. Far better in all departments, the guys from Panama City out-shot, out-rebounded, out-defensed the harmless, hapless team from Marianna, coasting to an easy 25 point half-time lead. Poor Joe DeChristoforo. He'd spent so much time and energy attempting to help form a half-way presentable basketball team, only to have it run into a real meat-grinder of an opponent, which was now soundly taking them to the woodshed. Even worse, in the fourth quarter Dick was literally knocked out of the game. This occurred in the following manner. He had been desperately trying to keep pace with a dribbler speeding up court on a fast break, Dick two steps behind him. Figuring the guy would try for a lay-up, Dick managed to finally come abreast of him, as they both headed for the basket. At the last second, Dick saw another white jersey out of the corner of his eye and, realizing the upcoming feed-off, was ready for the backhand pass his opponent would attempt. However, he hadn't correctly gauged either the timing or velocity of the pass. As a result, the sudden and well-spun pass hit him straight in the face, stunning him and knocking one of the lenses out of his glasses. Wobbling to the sidelines, angry and embarrassed, at having the smarts to know in advance that the behind-the-back pass was coming, but not possessing the skill to intercept it, instead, getting it flush in the face, making him look like an absolute simpleton, he thought, what an incredible display of ineptitude on his part!

Returning home, he found his brother in a foul mood, once again morosely reviewing the "pig roast" of last month, which, according to Jim, had renewed failed to live up to his expectations. The whole shindig was costing him and arm and leg, plus the time and effort he'd expended into organizing the event. Moreover, and now Jim came to the nexus of the matter, he had been so busy handling minor details the whole day, that he never really had the time to set down and jowl with all those friends milling around his house and garden, avidly gabbing with one another, while the host was constantly on the go. No, it just didn't make any dollars or sense, so Jim was seriously considering canceling next year's roast, asking Dick for his two bits. Not hesitating a second, Dick, corroborating his brother's doubts, told him frankly that he had come to the same conclusion, that the game wasn't worth the candle. To that, Jim added that Bruce, a friend of his, who had always done yeoman's duty in roasting the pig itself, had inadvertently slid into a bitter altercation between the two of them, resulting in a freeze in their relationship – another reason for calling quits to the yearly roast. Anyway, Jim, for years now, had been using his career with Social Security to slowly, but steadily, tack his way into the wind, his long-term goal being to settle down in Tallahassee; and now finally very close to realizing his goal, Marianna merely between a temporary station along the way.

Short Timer

The tersely worded missive from Taiwan made no bones about Li Shi's demand that he fish or cut bait regarding his too often postponed decision as to when to return to Taiwan, practically issuing an ultimatum, intimating she possessed a "significant other" in petto, should Dick, once again procrastinate. This letter represented the proverbial straw which broke the camel's back, forcing him to come to an immediate decision, something he was loathe to do, but knew that he would have to bite the bullet sooner or later anyway, so he sat down, replying on the spot to Li Shi's letter, stating that he was quitting his job at ACI and would thus be returning to Taiwan, probably toward the end of April. Satisfied to have finally gotten the monkey of his back, he walked into the living room to inform his brother about the decision made, somewhat surprised to hear Jim reply that he had sensed for weeks now that such a move was in the works, consequently taking everything in stride – knowing his brother was still locked into his phase of being a wandering star.

From the shocked expression on his face, Dick could tell that Mr. Sexton had been completely sandbagged by Dick's decision to terminate his work at ACI, leaving the education department suddenly bereft of a science teacher, meaning they'd have to scramble fast to find a suitable replacement. Dick made it clear that he held no umbrage against ACI, thankful for the opportunity for a unique chance to gain a semblance of understanding regarding the trials and tribulations of incarcerating young men for years at a time for crimes and various misdemeanors, while, simultaneously, attempting to educate them for future gainful occupations on the outside once they had been released. This as an answer in particular to the rather high rate of recidivism in Florida. Upon leaving the office, it suddenly occurred to Dick that since he'd merely had some six weeks left in the prison, well, he could let his hair just keep growing, not having to worry about seeing a barber. He also decided to not yet tell anyone about his decision to leave, postponing it until later.

At the beginning of March astounding events took place, with the Democratic candidate Jimmy Carter clearly winning both in Vermont (a New England state!) and in Florida, later adding Illinois and North Carolina to his skein, now have unequivocally proven that, although from the Deep South, he was a viable candidate nation-wide, the recent primary results making him a front-runner. Lunch time at ACI saw the candidate swamped with accolades, citing his southern roots, his military experience, his administrative capabilities, his openness and honesty; plus, above all, here was a true born-again Baptist, being accepted by wide swaths of the American voters, not only in the mid-west, but particularly in northern states! Some one hundred years after the bloody Civil War, the Deep South was returning to the United States, or as some wags put it, the rest of the US was becoming more "Dixiefied". Whatever; fact was that there was the distinct possibility that a southern Baptist might just be elected in November, and that thought alone sufficed to engender a storm of lunch time conversations and debates, many proclaimed themselves now avid supporters of "our Jimmeh".

Florida, geographically seen, is one long, long state. Not immediately visible to those traveling cross-state, say, from Orlando to Tampa, or for those milling around down on the Gold Coast, going perhaps from West Palm Beach to Miami. However, for those persons having to traverse almost the whole state, well, they begin to realize that the Sunshine State, from Pensacola to Key West, is basically Texas-wide and California-long. For those individuals and families wanting to visit their incarcerated sons, brothers, husbands out in the panhandle, this trip could be of a daunting nature, these persons often having to leave their homes before dawn, returning often late in the evenings, if not at night! Of course, those lucky enough to live in north Florida, a visit consisted merely of a few hours drive- a hop, skip and jump affair. The bulk of the state's population lay nonetheless in the central and southern parts. In fact, one could describe the swiftly growing urban structure of Florida as looking like an h written backwards, with the steam beginning in Jacksonville, reaching along the coast down to Miami. Starting from Daytona Beach, a branch snakes its way across the state through Orlando and Lakeland, then pivoting southward, following the Gulf coast down to Naples. Since the system of interstate highways was at that time only in the planning stage or incomplete, families often faced major logistical problems when motoring upstate, especially those from distant towns and cities.

That Friday in mid-March, Dick had been told that there were certain papers, documents awaiting his signature; and thus Mr. Sexton had asked him if he could see his way clear to making an exception and drive over on Sunday afternoon to take care of the matter. Having nothing else planned, Dick hopped into his Karmann Ghia, quickly speeding over to Sneads, thinking the process would merely be a matter of minutes, maybe five or ten, at the most. And right he was, with him ready to leave the admin building fifteen minutes after his arrival - or so he thought. Upon coming out of the main office, he saw a room, off to his side, crowded with inmates and visitors. What an amazing amalgam of the human condition met his eyes. A complete compendium of emotions on full display; persons hugging one another, crying (some almost hysterically), while others were smiling, laughing, much as if on a family picnic. A few were even involved in a shouting match, hurling expletives at one another, until the guards intervened to cool things down. Over in the far corner, Dick spotted one of his students sitting alone, quietly talking with his young wife, who held their child in her arms. My Lord, she looked every bit of being under 20 – and already lumbered with a tiny tot plus the father being in prison. Unobserved, Dick riveted his attention on his student, who was now speaking softly to his wife, obviously attempting to calm her fears and provide some glimmer of hope for the coming months. The young man's wan face spoke volumes in itself, radiating his despondency, best expressed by his sad eyes, constantly caressing his wife and child. A whole room full of such an emotional squalor.

Lost in his thoughts, Dick suddenly felt a hand placed lightly on his shoulder. Turning around, he recognized the beaming face of "Earl the Pearl", both surprised to see each other on this Sunday afternoon. Without much ado, Earl invited him into the room to meet his mother and aunt who had motored all the way over from Tallahassee to visit him, with his mom having come all the way down from Philadelphia, spending the night at her sister's house in Frenchtown. Once again, Dick figured he knew the source of Earl's insouciance, his innate light-heartedness, which provided the young man with the considerable ability to roll with the punches fate had ordained, his seemingly non-chalance at life's inequities, the probable reasons sitting there in front of him. The two women radiated warmth, empathy, all bound up in a caring, but simultaneously common sense fashion. Earl's mom told him that she had a job lined up for him as soon as he returned home after his EOS, everyone eager to see him again, and her certain that he'd be walking the straight and narrow in years to come. From what Dick had gleaned from his occasional conversations with Earl, it seemed as if his hopes of making it after his release were well-founded and, not as in the cases of so many other inmates, merely straws in the wind, ephemeral at best, so often based on an unbelievable solid foundation of blatant self-deception, impenetrable against all rational thought. On his drive back to Marianna, Dick ruminated over the events just transpired, chastising himself for not being able to do something more *practicable* in aiding his students, not just in an academic sense, but, to put it more succinctly, getting them *out* of prison and back *into* civilian life. Little did he know that an opportunity lay just around the corner.

Some days later, as one of his classes ended, Billy Ray Almond asked if he could remain after the other inmates had left, stating that he needed to talk with with his teacher about a pressing problem which had just arisen. Billy Ray was a local, from the Panhandle area, a rather short, stout student, consistent in his efforts to obtain his GED, rather quiet and studious, thus Dick was convinced that a talk with Billy might just enhance his academic performance even further, seeing that the test itself was due in a month or two. Much to his surprise, the conversation took a much different turn:

Dick: "Now, Billy Ray, just what can I do for you? Need some help preparing for the upcoming GED?"

Billy Ray: "No sir, not exactly. It's that something unexpected has turned up."

Dick: "You're not in any trouble, are you? Problems with other inmates?"

Billy Ray: "No, none of that. Yesterday I had a meeting with Mr. Duncan concerning my overall progress at ACI."

Dick: "And, what did he have to say?"

Billy Ray: "Well, he was very satisfied with my progress, stating that my EOS was in no danger. In fact, he told me that he had met with Mr. Sexton and other staff members, with all agreeing that, if I could find a job, they were even considering an early release."

Dick: "So?"

Billy Ray (plaintively): "But how can I find a job while I'm in prison?"

Immediately Dick saw that the inmate was trapped in a true *Catch 22* situation. He could be released if he found gainful employment, but how was he to realize this while imprisoned? The offer, certainly well-intended, was devilish in its implications.

Dick: "So, why are you telling me this. Where do I fit in?"

Billy Ray: "Mr. Mann, I would like you to do me a really big favor."

Dick: "Yeah, and that is?"

Billy Ray: "Well, I used to work as a construction worker over in Panama City. I was always in good terms with the boss and, well, I think, I hope that if you'd give him a phone call, explaining my situation, he'd be glad to help me out."

Dick: "Do you have his telephone number on you?"

Billy Ray: "No, but I can get it. (Pause). Would you being willing to make the call?"

Dick: (slowly): "Well, I know one thing, I can sure as well try, so get me the number."

Billy Ray (jubilant): "Oh, I *will*! Thank you very much for your help!"

Dick: "Let's see if we can get you out of this hole."

A week later Dick received the phone number of Mr. Landsdale, who ran a construction firm in Panama City. Before making the call, Dick felt some trepidations; was this legal, was he guilty of aiding a single inmate, why was he helping a white kid from the panhandle, when their were so many other inmates deserving his aid too? Just as during his last months of active duty in the Navy he had developed a real *short-timer's* attitude, the same phenomenon occurred here too, with him now determined to do at least something to assuage his conscience, confident, in the final analysis, that he was *doing the right thing*. At the beginning, Mr. Landesdale appeared a bit ruffled at the call, with him not sure of the intent; however, as Dick delivered more details, the man seemed to increasingly gain interest. After thanking Dick for his efforts on Billy Ray's behalf, the boss said that he'd definitely phone ACI to see what could be done. Sure enough, a few days later Billy Ray strolled into the classroom, a big grin plastered all over his face, announcing that he would be released the very next day, thanking Dick for all his efforts. That night he and Jim had a cold beer, toasting to a small, but signal victory, a modicum of justice, at least for one happy inmate.

Through the grapevine, he discerned that the administration was having a difficult time in finding an adequate replacement for him, with the position of a Classroom II teacher not particularly popular, due to the salary, working conditions and the fact that the institution found itself up in Florida's armpit, a long fifty mile drive over from Tallahassee; or, if one wanted to save on gas and rent, find satisfaction in the bucolic life style in small towns such as Chattahoochee, Blountstown or Marianna. Just a week before Dick was scheduled to leave, Mr. Sexton barged into one of the morning classes with Dick's successor in tow, a slim, tight-lipped Mr. Barrow, who, from the looks of him, had taken the job as science teacher as a last, desperate measure. Carefully sizing

the young man up, Dick estimated that his academic background sufficed, however, in judging his attitude toward the inmates, he figured
that the new teacher, much like Dick himself, would have to weather
the stormy weeks ahead as best he could, since Dick noticed some of
the bolder inmates smiling slightly, winking to one another, as if to say:
"Let's see if we can pull this guy's chain". Clem Barrow certainly knew a
life-preserver when he saw it, for just like Dick had some fifteen
months beforehand, Clem thankfully grasped the academic program
set up by Mr. Nielson, Dick's predecessor, with its carefully constructed
series of written multiple-choice questions for each chapter of the science textbook. Returning to the classroom quickly after lunch, Dick
gave Clem a run-down on those rules he had implemented to instill a
certain amount of discipline in the classes, stressing the fact that the
teacher always had that threat of "lock-up" to use against recalcitrant
individuals, should push come to shove. However, Dick mentioned
being proud to never have had to use this ultimate weapon, while at the
same time honestly admitting that he had come close to using it a couple of times. The next few days, he allowed Clem to go around the
classroom, helping different inmates with their answer sheets, trying to
get the new teacher and inmates used to each other, figuring that this
immediate proximity would serve to allay any uncalled for hostility on
the part of the inmates. Occasionally, he'd hear the faint, but audible
clicks of the speaker above the blackboard, telling him that Mr. Sexton
was surreptitiously eavesdropping on the class, wanting to confirm
confidence that all was well.

During the last week he also received a letter from his friend Helmut in
West Berlin wishing him a fruitful sojourn on Taiwan and mentioning
that a friend of his had reserved a room for Dick at the 国际学舍
(The International Student House), with Dick fully confident of both
finding housing plus a job through his Chinese friends from 1973-74.
Moreover, he had saved enough money to see him through the first
months, plus now being able to make himself understood in Chinese.

Four days before leaving Marianna he received a phone call from Doziers asking him if he had time to come out for a job interview. With a certain lilt in his voice, he told the folks at Dozier they were "a day late, and a dollar short" with their offer because he had just finished a stint of teaching out at Apalachee, with the job offer unfortunately coming fifteen months too late. Now he was headed westward in the direction of Taiwan, so, thanks, but no thanks. Afterward, he drove down to the Jackson County Health Center for his vaccinations against smallpox, cholera and typhoid.

Throughout the long drive over to Tallahassee, he began a slow review the past fifteen months. A whole kaleidoscope of images flashed in a semi-chronologisch fashion through his mind, a melange of memories, good and bad, defeats, victories, unexpected setbacks, new insights gained, the slowly dawning knowledge of his own limits, his lack of "real life" knowledge caused by too much "book learning", as had often been intimated, directly or not, from those hot, sweaty days of working in the orange groves in central Florida back in the summer of 1963, or those co-workers at ACI, who were either smiling or groaning at his innocent naiveté, at his incongruous attempts to imply that he knew the dao, the righteous path. He, the outsider, parachuted one ungodly day into their midst, smack-dab in Jackson county with its pick-ups, guns and God- fearing folk, and with this young whipper-snapper, who had studied in Berlin and Taiwan and thought himself anointed to convert the locals into his own brand of European "socialism", which seemed to the locals much as if he were attempting to saddle a cow. What a typical case of, here today, gone tomorrow – such as was always expected of such a lightweight!

It must have been around the time he went through Grand Ridge that he felt the first discomforting signs – a slight headache perhaps, a feeling of dizziness? By the time he crossed the bridge over the Chattahoochee he realized that the three inoculations were belatedly having pernicious side-effects, forcing him to really concentrate on driving.

One thought in particular spooked about in his mind, the same one he had felt the night of his graduation from high school, of a door silently being closed behind him, never more to be reopened. For this meant too, that those fifteen months at ACI were gone, merely history, non-accessible, this pivotal period of this life forever past, leaving him with brief, but deep feeling of sadness, of loss. Caught up in this maelstrom of emotions, he mulled over the death of his good friend, who cruelly had taken three innocent victims along with him. Shortly thereafter, one of his own students bled to death when stabbed during an altercation among inmates. Then, topping it off, his student with a known heart-problem, complaining of feeling ill, was told to run a lap or face being locked up. A decision that had cost a life. All this within the span of seven months!

Driving through Quincy, he noticed that he was beginning to sweat, plus running a light fever, feeling a bit queasy. All these unpleasant symptoms tended to stoke a furious review, not merely of the past months, but of his all too precarious plans for the future, all shot down in flames upon his return to the states. Those inchoate ideas quickly dissolving under the harsh glare of reality, now leading him to simply kick the can further down the road, trying his best to make a decision by indecision, as if a brilliant solution to his dilemma would suddenly appear – *deus ex machina* – literally out of nowhere. However, he wasn't the only one with problems. Jim was still desperately attempting to escape from Marianna, aiming for a position in Tallahassee (like so many others), Dan was encountering difficulties in his internship at the Flagship Bank down in Miami, whereas Dave, twenty miles north in Ft. Lauderdale, was, much to his dismay, discovering that his father-in-law showed little inclination to retire after showing his daughter and son-in-law the ropes of running a wholesale grocery business. Doug ensconced in his spacious office, was still researching for Florida Retirement, doing his level best "not to make any waves", as his boss succinctly put it. Occasionally in his trance-like condition, Dick, remembering the recent phone call from Dozier's, ruminated on what might have happen had he ended up working out at the reform school instead of ACI. Although he realized the proximity of the school would have provided him a great saving of time, in retrospect, he was belatedly thankful for his hard-earned experiences at the state prison, convinced that Dozier's would have certainly been the easier route, ACI, the more difficult obstacle to surmount. When attempting to recapitulate his time working at the prison, he thought back to that cartoon character his brother Dave had shown him in the Tampa Tribune. A small possum named Pogo, who lived in the Okeefenokee swamp, who was always coming up with pithy quotes, one of which had remained etched in Dick's brain. Alluding to Oliver Hazard Perry, Pogo had turned the quote around 180° degrees, stating that "we have met the enemy and he is *us*".

By the time he had reached the outskirts of Tallahassee, Dick, now sweating profusely, flirted with loosing control of the vehicle. When stopping for a car entering the street from his right, he suddenly stepped on the gas pedal, almost ramming the car crossing in front of him, with the driver cursing him for almost causing an accident. Now fully aware of his precarious state, Dick drove the last three miles to Doug's house at a slow, steady pace, not wanting to risk another such incident, gripping the steering wheel tightly, eyes focused the the road. Arriving safe and sound, he immediately crashed for the whole afternoon, hoping, as he sailed off into a deep sleep, that the effects of the vaccinations would wear off within the next 24 hours.

Luckily for him, he was able to get up for supper, returning shortly afterwards back to his bed, where he slept the whole night through. The next morning after breakfast saw him checking his luggage and going over his flight itinerary: Tallahassee -Atlanta, change planes, Atlanta – Houston – Las Vegas -San Francisco, change planes, San Francisco – Honolulu – Tokyo – Taipei. Wow, practically halfway round the world. Doug kindly drove him out to the airport, wishing him a good flight, adding he hoped to see Dick again in the foreseeable future.

As the Delta flight banked steeply to the right, he peered out the window, hoping, in vain, to somehow be able to discern a view of the area around Chattahoochee on that late spring morning, which saw the sky already chock-a-block with those small, cumulus cotton balls, effectively blocking his attempts to see further than ten miles. Some twenty minutes later, a person in the row ahead of him (obviously a frequent flyer) happen to mention that that he thought he could roughly make out Plains, just west of Americus. Just the mention of that small town started Dick thinking. Imagine if that local boy, the Annapolis midshipman, the peanut farmer, that born-again Christian, could actually succeed in winning the nomination as the presidential candidate of the Democratic party. What if he were to be elected President of the United States?! Merely the thought alone sent his mind flying off on a tangent. Why, why that would mean, one hundred and ten years after the bloody Civil War, that the South would once again become part and parcel of the whole country, no longer being an economic and political backwater of the nation. What a boon that would be for all citizens living the Deep South. Well, this was all theory right now; nonetheless, Jimmy kept winning a growing number of primary elections.

Sipping on his glass of Dr. Pepper offered to him by the cute stewardess, Dick turned his thoughts toward the immediate future. Contrary to his arrival in Taipei in the fall of 1973, he now had plenty of cash for the coming months, plus enough knowledge of the Chinese language to cover everyday exigencies. Moreover, he also had a temporary lodging at the International House, him being confident of finding an apartment to share with other students. As for the crucial question of where this all was leading to, well, in his let-the-chips-fall-where-they-may attitude, he was determined to cross that bridge when he came to it. In the last few years, his life had become a series of unexpected setbacks, turns, surprises, all causing him to deviate sharply from his intended course. Slightly unsettled by this seemingly endless skein of *quo vadis* queries, he pulled down the shade on his window, closing his eyes, hoping for a quick visit by Morpheus.

Epilogue

I n German, the phrase *Glück im Unglück*, means that the person involved has had luck in his misfortune. As the year 1975 commenced, the author, much to his chagrin, learned that he was not to be offered a position as a teacher at the Dozier School for Boys just outside of Marianna, due to certain "difficulties" within the establishment, thus being forced to accept an alternative employment at the state prison some twenty miles away. The ugly thought of having to teach at the far away *prison*, instead of a nearby *boy's school*, seemed to him thoroughly distasteful; it remained however, the only viable solution.

Little did he know that he had, by sheer luck, avoided the poison chalice being passed around at the time. Forty-four years later, he was shocked to discover a book written by the Pulitzer Prize winning author, Colson Whitehead. In his book entitled *The Nickel Boys*, Whitehead described the egregious conditions at the school and the cruelty with which the boys were treated. Although the characters in the book are fictitious, they are obviously based on true experiences, suffered by many other victims over the span of decades. In retrospect, the author has realized, belatedly, his fortune in having had to choose to teach over at the state prison, now fully aware of what terrible moral maelstrom had been just narrowly avoided.